"We got a note from Dragon Precinct."

Sergeant Jonas shuffled through his parchments. "One of their informants said that two halflings, a barbarian, a priest, and three warrior-types—human, elf, and dwarf—all took rooms in the Dog and Duck and had dinner together."

Danthres leaned back in her wooden chair and groaned. "Lord and Lady, not another heroic quest."

"I'm afraid so," Jonas said gravely.

Torin grinned and looked over to Danthres. "Two coppers says that our next call is from the Dog and Duck."

"No bet," Danthres said. "But three coppers says it's a bar brawl."

"You're on."

Almost as if on cue, a guard ran in. "We got a body."

Danthres asked, "Where?"

"Dog and Duck, ma'am. One of the guests."

With a look at Torin, she asked, "Bar brawl?"

The guard shook his head. "No, ma'am. Cleaning lady found a dead body in a room."

Torin was grinning again. "That'll be three coppers."

Ignoring him, she said, "Let's go."

KEITH R.A. DECANDIDO

POCKET STAR BOOKS
New York London Toronto Sydney

This book is a work of fiction. Names, characters, places and incidents are products of the author's imagination or are used fictitiously. Any resemblance to actual events or locales or persons, living or dead, is entirely coincidental.

An *Original* Publication of POCKET BOOKS

A Pocket Star Book published by
POCKET BOOKS, a division of Simon & Schuster, Inc.
1230 Avenue of the Americas, New York, NY 10020

For information address Pocket Books, 1230 Avenue of the Americas, New York, NY 10020

ISBN: 0-7434-6770-1

First Pocket Books printing August 2004

10 9 8 7 6 5 4 3 2 1

Cover design by Patrick Kang
Illustration by Romas Kukalis

Manufactured in the United States of America

For information regarding special discounts for bulk purchases, please contact Simon & Schuster Special Sales at 1-800-456-6798 or business@simonandschuster.com

To the Forebearance:
The Mom, The Dad, The Party Vegetable,
and The Tall Fuzzy One.
I finally did it.

ACKNOWLEDGMENTS

Special thanks to John J. Ordover, my editor, who took the chance; Lucienne Diver, my agent, who more than earned her percentage; Scott Shannon, the publisher, who gave support above and beyond; Elisa Kassin and Jessica McGivney, the in-house editorial folk, who kept the paperwork mills grinding as fast as they could; the Forebearance, for all the many many years of love and encouragement; CITH, my writers group, for making the work so much better; the Malibu gang and the Geek Patrol, for over a decade (and counting!) of overall goofiness; Laura Anne Gilman, for more reasons than I can count; and Marcus and Mittens, the cats, for the love that only a couple of fuzzy affection sluts can provide.

Thanks also to the multitude of writers, ranging from J.R.R. Tolkien to David Simon, who provided inspiration for this most peculiar tale.

But most of all, thanks to Terri Osborne, the love of my life, for all of everything.

Prologue

Gan Brightblade's last thoughts before his neck was broken were about how happy he was.

Dinner had been one of the most enjoyable experiences of recent times, even if the food itself was somewhat lacking. The Dog and Duck Inn may have suited his group's needs in terms of accommodation during their brief layover in Cliff's End, but its kitchen left much to be desired. The meat was bland, the drinks weak, and the vegetables limp.

But the company—ah, the company was what mattered.

For the past five weeks, he had traveled on horseback with the group of comrades-in-arms Brother Genero had gathered at the Temisan monastery in Velessa. The trip to Cliff's End had been mostly uneventful, leavened only by brief encounters with the usual bandits and trolls, plus some young fool of a magic-user. He wasn't even registered with the Brotherhood of Wizards, probably as much due to his lack of talent as anything. Defeating him was the work of a few minutes. Bogg had wanted to kill him, of course, and did cut off the top of the boy's ear, but Genero insisted that he live, as he was more misguided than evil.

Typical priest, Gan had thought. Besides, the Brotherhood didn't tolerate unregistered magic-users for very long. They would deal with the boy in short order.

Upon arrival, they stabled their horses on the outskirts of town, then proceeded into the crowded city on foot. Cliff's End had never been Gan's favorite place to visit, though he was always impressed with the variety of people he found within its borders. Rich and poor, human and dwarf, mage and priest, elf and gnome—all you had to do was stand still on any of Cliff's End's numerous thoroughfares, and you'd encounter every type of person in Flingaria ere long. If, for some reason, one type didn't pass you by, all you had to do was go to the docks, and one would likely be in on the next boat.

Gan and his friends checked into this dreary inn in the center of the city-state, for expediency's sake as much as anything. It was large enough to accommodate them, ordinary enough to minimize the fuss that would be made over them, close enough to the docks so that securing sea passage the next day would be easy, but not so close to that part of town that they risked an infectious disease or six just by walking around. Bogg, of course, cared little for the latter, but Gan and Olthar insisted on at least a modicum of cleanliness.

They had dinner together, ostensibly to plan strategy, but they wound up whiling away the hours regaling the other patrons with tales of their exploits. Ubàrlig spoke of liberating the human slave camps of the western elves. Bogg told cruder tales of his fights against the trolls that menaced his village in the north, and the women who vied for his affections in the aftermath of that battle. Inevitably, and even though everyone knew the story, Olthar was asked to tell of his betrayal of his aunt, the Elf Queen, during the elven wars, which led to a permanent exile from his own people but victory for King Marcus and Queen Marta. Only Genero—out of typical priestly modesty—and the halfling twins—for fear of being incriminated in acts of dubious legality—kept quiet.

Gan himself told of his days as a young soldier thirty years before, when he was among the forces who helped overthrow Chalmraik the Foul. What he did not say—nor did anyone else—was that Genero had gathered them all together because the priest had received a vision from Temisa that Chalmraik was about to rise again. The powerful wizard once ruled over half of Flingaria, and Genero could not let that happen again.

Unfortunately, his warnings to the Brotherhood

had fallen on deaf ears. Instead, Genero brought together all his old comrades-in-arms. In the morning, Gan and Genero planned to hire a boat to take them to the island where Chalmraik was hatching his latest plan, so they could do what the Brotherhood would not.

Soon enough, the night's revelry ended, and Gan trudged up the stairs to the decently furnished room the Dog and Duck had provided for him.

As he removed his mail, sword, and tunic and tossed them on the bed, Gan smiled. He was with good comrades who would soon join him in a noble quest to rid Flingaria of its greatest curse once and for all. In a lifetime filled with great deeds and greater triumphs, this would be the perfect capper.

One minute later, he lay dead on the floor of his room, his head at an impossible angle.

In the morning, his body was found by the Dog and Duck's cleaning woman, who arrived early to tidy the room in the hopes of getting a glance at the great hero Gan Brightblade. It took half a minute for her to stop screaming—and by then, the Cliff's End Castle Guard had been summoned.

One

"What are you doing here?"

Lieutenant Danthres Tresyllione of the Cliff's End Castle Guard asked the question of her partner, Lieutenant Torin ban Wyvald. She was being confronted by a sight she'd never seen in their ten years of partnership: Torin arriving in the office before her. The only times he'd ever even gotten in at the same time as her was when they came together. Otherwise, he was always late for their twelve-hour shift.

"I work here," Torin said in reply, the white teeth of his wide grin shining through his thick red beard. The beard obscured most of Torin's face, as did his mane of red hair, which extended past his shoulders. All Danthres could truly see were his long, aquiline nose and his twinkling green eyes. Early on in their partnership, she had realized that, no matter what Torin's mood might have been, his eyes always had an amused look, as if he knew a joke that he wasn't quite ready to share with the rest of the world.

"That is the rumor, yes."

As Danthres spoke, a seven-peal chime rang all around them in the air, marking the time as seven in the morning, and the official start of the day shift, which would last until nineteen. The Brotherhood of Wizards had set up the timekeeping system, as well as the spell that rang out each hour with what everyone referred to as the "time-chimes." Danthres had never understood why they codified it so that the day began in the middle of the night—sunup made much more sense to her, especially since their shifts were concurrent with the rise and fall of the sun. She had added that to the ever-growing list of things that annoyed her about the practice of magic.

While the chimes rang, the other four detectives in their shift entered from either the west-wall door, which connected the squad room to the rest of the castle, or from the pantry. Danthres gave Lieutenants Dru, Hawk, and Iaian a nod each. She didn't bother to acknowledge Iaian's partner, Amilar Grovis, as doing so might lead to actual conversation with the young lieutenant, something that was guaranteed to turn her stomach.

Torin said, "I had to deal with a domestic."

Danthres frowned. "You got a call? Why wasn't I—?"

"I didn't say I got a call, I said I had to *deal with*

a domestic. The couple downstairs have taken their arguments to a new level—and a new time frame. I was woken out of a sound sleep three hours before sunup by their fighting, which involved both screaming and the throwing of breakable objects."

Smiling, Danthres asked, "Did you bring them in?"

"No, but I made several threats along those lines should they ever wake me up again."

"Given what you're like first thing in the morning, that probably included a great deal of growling."

"Indeed." Torin's grin returned. "Let's hope it works."

"You know, you could just move in with me and be done with it. I certainly have the space." As she spoke, Danthres removed her brown cloak and hung it on a peg between the one holding Torin's own cloak and the empty one that Hawk never used, preferring to drape his cloak on his chair. The earth color symbolized their rank, with the gryphon crest of Lord Albin and Lady Meerka showing that they were assigned to the headquarters of the Guard, located in the eastern wing of the castle at the outskirts of Cliff's End, the city-state that constituted the Lord and Lady's demesne. Danthres liked the color, as it held dirt well.

"Danthres, we see each other *at least* twelve hours a day. I like the idea of having a place of my own."

"Well, at least come home with me tonight, spare yourself the bickering neighbors."

Torin laughed his hearty laugh. "I think I've sufficiently intimidated them into quiet for a few days, at least. But I may still take you up on that offer." He stood up from the large wooden desk that the partners shared, gathering up a dozen or so scrolls. "In any event, I thought I would take advantage of the opportunity to finish off some paperwork."

Danthres took her own seat, which was on the opposite side of the desk from Torin's. She watched as he walked past the other two desks in the squad room, one occupied by Dru and Hawk, the other by Iaian and Grovis, to the window that took up most of the north wall.

"The Marvilk case." In response to Torin's words, the window shimmered and twisted, changing from a view of the Forest of Nimvale that Danthres had long since grown bored with to that of a bearded male face. This was Ep, the imp in charge of the extradimensional storage area where all the Guard's files were stored, and Danthres's least favorite Guard employee.

"You know, you really don't need to tell me where the files are supposed to go," Ep said in his reedy voice. "Just send the scrolls through, I'll figure out which file to put them in by reading them."

"I thought I'd save you the trouble," Torin said politely. "After all, you're a busy imp." He placed the scrolls in the imp's beard, which also served as the gateway to the file room.

Ep sighed, an odd action coming from a face-shaped window. "I do appreciate the consideration, I suppose. At least you're nice about it, unlike your partner."

"I heard that," Danthres said.

"You were meant to."

Before Danthres could reply, the face reshaped itself back into an ordinary window. She shook her head. "Little bastard. He'll probably put them in with the triple murder."

Torin shrugged. "Probably, but at least I made the effort."

He crossed the room to the south wall, which was free of interdimensional portals, sticking with more mundane doors that Danthres, and the other detectives, had far greater use for: the three interrogation rooms and the pantry.

The latter room was Torin's destination. "I'm going to see if any good pastries are left." Sergeant Jonas's wife always baked for the day shift, but usually only the soggiest fare was left by the time Torin arrived, so Danthres couldn't blame him for wanting to take advantage of this rare opportunity. "Want any?"

"No thanks. I passed Corin's stand on the way in, and he's *still* grateful to us for catching that thief, so I'm laden with biscuits." She grinned. "Consider it another incentive to come home with me tonight."

Laughing, Torin continued to the pantry.

"It's disgusting, you know," said a nasal voice from behind her.

Scowling, Danthres turned to look at Grovis, who was walking over from the desk he shared with Iaian. His goggle-eyed face framed by mousy brown hair, Grovis looked even stupider than usual by virtue of the pastry crumbs around his mouth.

Danthres snarled. "What is?"

"You two associating—fornicating like that. That sort of behavior is an affront to Ghandurha." He made several hand gestures that Ghandurha-worshipers used to ward off evil. "Especially a human with an elf—disgusting."

"I'll have to find some way to live with your god's disappointment, Grovis." Danthres turned her attention to the piles of parchment on her half of the desk. Torin's actions this morning reminded her of how far behind she herself was on her own paperwork. The alternative was to remind Grovis that her very existence was due to a liaison between an elven man and a human woman. *I'd rather drive a wooden stake through my tongue than talk to him any more than necessary.*

Before Grovis could continue his own thoughts on the subject of Ghandurha's views on sex, Sergeant Jonas entered the room from the west-wall door. Grovis sat back down at his desk.

Jonas shuffled half a dozen parchments, his green cloak billowing behind him. The gray-haired veteran always seemed to be moving about one and a half times as fast as everyone else. Dru once speculated that he'd purchased a Speed Spell from the Brotherhood of Wizards, but Hawk pointed out that he could never afford such a spell on a sergeant's salary.

The sergeant surveyed the three desks and six chairs, noting that one of the latter was empty. "I see everyone's here except ban Wyvald, as usual."

"Wrong, I'm afraid." Torin reentered from the pantry as he spoke those words, powdered sugar adding white to the red of his beard.

"This is why you're not a detective, Jonas," Grovis said archly. "Never come to conclusions without all the facts."

Danthres noticed Iaian, sitting across from Grovis, rolling his rheumy eyes to the heavens, as he often did when his young partner opened his mouth.

Not even sparing Grovis a glance, Jonas turned to Dru and Hawk. "Any luck with our rapist?"

Hawk shook his head, causing his waist-length dreadlocks to bounce. "Boneen give us a better description this time, and we give it to all'a sergeants at all'a precincts, but ain't nothin' yet."

Torin asked, "Why was this one better?"

"Gettin' overconfident—didn't wear a mask this time."

"That was foolish."

Angrily, Danthres said, "He's gotten away with six rapes."

Scratching his pale cheek, Dru said, "Well, c'mon, I mean, being able to walk through walls makes him *real* hard to capture."

Hawk added, "We lookin' into the local shops, seein' if anyone's sellin' Walk Through Walls Spells. Nothin' so far."

Jonas dipped his quill in the inkwell on Dru and Hawk's desk and made a note on his parchment. "What about the Brotherhood?" he asked, which prompted several snorts of derision.

Holding up a piece of parchment from his desk, Dru read from it. "'The Brotherhood of Wizards has sold no such spells within the period requested.' Like that means a damn thing."

Earnestly, Grovis said, "The Brotherhood is a noble and august organization that has regulated the use of magic since the days of Chalmraik the Foul. They deserve our respect."

Dru made a noise that was halfway between a laugh and a snort. "If they were *really* so shit-hot at regulating, our caseload'd be cut in half. It's harder to find a good whore in this town than black-market magic."

Primly, Grovis said, "I'm sure that you're wrong about that."

"Speaking of black-market magic," Jonas said to Grovis before Dru could reply, "where are we on our fake-glamour ring?"

"We're on the cusp of an arrest, I'm sure of it," Grovis said with a confidence that didn't extend to the expression on Iaian's face.

The older lieutenant said, "We've got some leads, nothing solid."

Jonas pursed his lips. "Captain's getting pressure from the Brotherhood on this one. It should've been put down days ago."

Iaian shrugged. "They're better than we thought. If the Brotherhood has a problem, let *them* deal with it. They're supposed to be the ones who regulate the use of magic, after all," he added with a withering gaze at his partner.

Ignoring the jab, Grovis said, "We will close the case, *Sergeant*, and I'll thank you not to take such a tone."

"You're welcome," Jonas said dryly. He turned to Torin and Danthres. "You two are up next, right?"

Danthres nodded. "Unless the magistrate needs more for that triple murder."

"Good." Jonas shuffled through his parchments. "We got a note from Dragon Precinct. One of their informants said that two halflings, a barbarian, a priest, and three warrior types—one human, one elven, one dwarven—all took rooms in the Dog and Duck and had dinner together."

Danthres leaned back in her wooden chair and groaned. "Lord and Lady, not another heroic quest."

"I'm afraid so," Jonas said gravely. "Dragon's been told to keep a special eye on them. Those types *always* get into brawls."

"Or worse," Iaian said. "I remember that group that wiped out the Boar's Head Inn."

"I don't know that inn," Grovis said.

"You wouldn't, boy." Iaian chuckled. "Even if

someone like you would be caught dead in a place like that, it got burned to the ground before you were born."

Jonas said, "Last thing we want is a repeat of last year."

"What happened last year?" Grovis asked.

Patiently, Iaian explained. "Someone started a rumor about a dragon in the cliffs. We had a run of men with boiling blood and shit for brains coming through Cliff's End, each thinking *he'd* be the one to take it down." Iaian let loose with a rare, gap-toothed smile. "I think we set a record for assault calls that year."

Torin grinned, and he looked at Danthres. "Two coppers says that our next call is from the Dog and Duck."

"No bet," Danthres said. "But three coppers says it's a bar brawl."

"You're on."

Almost as if on cue, a guard ran in. He wore no cloak, but he was clad in the same leather armor emblazoned with the gryphon crest as the rest of them. "We got a body."

Jonas looked at Danthres and Torin. "All yours."

"Joy of joys," Torin said as he got up and moved toward the pegs that held his and Danthres's cloaks.

Danthres asked the guard, "Where?"

"Dog and Duck, ma'am. One of the guests."

With a look at Torin, she asked, "Bar brawl?"

The guard shook his head. "Not according to the

informant, ma'am. Said the cleaning lady found a dead body in a room."

Torin was grinning again as he handed Danthres her brown cloak. "That'll be three coppers."

Ignoring him, she said, "Let's go."

Danthres and Torin traveled on foot to the Dog and Duck, located in the heart of Dragon Precinct, the business district and middle-class region of town. Danthres, who had never gotten along with any horse she'd attempted to ride, had no problem with this. There really wasn't any other way to traverse the city-state, particularly once you got out of the mansion-laden portions of Unicorn Precinct. Horse-drawn supply wagons did come through, but at a slug's pace.

The previous Guard captain, an idiot named Brisban, did have a problem with it, unlike Danthres. Then again, he also had a problem with Danthres, but that solved itself when the captain died of a lung infection. Before his death, he had tried having the patrol guards do so on horseback so they could, as Brisban put it, "pursue malefactors more efficiently." However, the horses were only able to move as fast as the slowest pedestrians without the risk of trampling, which pretty much defeated the whole point of the exercise. Walking had remained the primary mode of travel within the Cliff's End city limits. Besides Danthres, this state of affairs also pleased the owners of the dozens of stables on the outskirts of the city-state.

Danthres had last been to the Dog and Duck three years ago, when a suspect in a murder was staying there. Since then, it had been refurbished—at least, that was how it seemed as she looked through the large crowd that had gathered around the outside, barely held in check by three guards wearing the Dragon crest on their leather armor. If nothing else, the wooden sign that hung from a small pole over the front door was newer and fancier. Where it used to be a crude painting of the two animals for which the inn was named, now much more sophisticated renderings of a canine and a waterfowl were carved directly into the wood.

Another guard was standing at the perimeter of the crowd, and walked briskly over to meet Danthres and Torin. After a moment, Danthres recognized him as Jared, one of the brighter guards assigned to Dragon—which meant that he could occasionally, if absolutely necessary, form a complex sentence.

"Mornin', Lieutenants. C'mon, I'll get you two inside."

"What've we got?" Torin asked as the guard started pushing the gawkers aside to clear a path so the two lieutenants could actually reach the front door.

"Y'ever hear of a guy named Gan Brightblade?"

"Who hasn't?" Torin said, sounding impressed.

"Me," Danthres said, totally unimpressed. "Who is he?"

Sparing Danthres an incredulous look as he pushed two tall men aside, Jared said, "He's one'a the greatest heroes of our time, ma'am."

"I think Captain Osric served under him once, in the old days," Torin added, referring to the current Guard captain, who had replaced Brisban. "He's dead?"

"Yes, sir."

Remembering the report, Danthres asked, "But not in a bar brawl?"

"No, ma'am."

"You're not getting out of those three coppers, Danthres," Torin said.

Most of the crowd's utterings were white noise to Danthres. Years of living in the cacophony of Cliff's End trained her to ignore most background noise for her sanity's sake, as the elven half of her heritage gave her above-average hearing. But she did catch comments here and there: "Gan Brightblade's dead!" "I hear tell 'twas those damned elves!" "Nah, it was Chalmraik the Foul! I heard 'em talkin' about 'im!" "Chalmraik's dead!" "Guard'll take care'a it." "Guard's a buncha shitbrains!" "*You're* a shitbrain!" And so on.

The noise died down as they crossed the threshold and Jared closed the large wooden door behind them. Danthres saw that the lobby remained more or less unchanged after three years, except perhaps that it was cleaner and there were a few more cushions against the wall. At present, the space was empty. Directly in front of her, parallel to the back wall of the room, was a large wooden desk, on which sat a fairly elaborate eagle quill that Danthres pegged as a total fake, a battered old ledger, an unnecessarily brightly polished bell, and an inkwell. Behind the desk was a pegboard, about half taken up with keys, and a doorway covered in a curtain, which Danthres assumed led to some kind of staff-only back room. To her left was the staircase leading up to the rooms on the second floor; to the right, the wide entrance to the bar/dining area. Danthres could only see partly into the latter—along with the kitchen and storage area that serviced it, the dining area took up almost the entirety of the ground floor—but what she saw were several people seated on the benches at the long wooden tables, who were more subdued than one would expect from patrons in a bar. Several guards from Dragon were visible around the perimeter of the room, as well.

"I assume," Danthres said, indicating the dining area, "that the patrons have all been gathered in there?"

Jared nodded. "Except for a few we let go back to their rooms, yes, ma'am."

Danthres put her head in her gloved hand. "Go upstairs—take a couple of the bigger guards with you—and get *everyone* out of their rooms. Assuming, of course, they haven't already jumped out the window and lost themselves in that mob out there.

No one is allowed upstairs who isn't employed by the Guard, is that clear?"

Nodding so enthusiastically Danthres thought his head would fall off—*which would not noticeably depreciate his brain power*, she thought—Jared moved toward the staircase.

"After you do that," Torin called to him, "send someone back to Dragon—Sergeant Grint's still running the day shift, yes?"

Jared smiled. "Unless the old bastard's choked on his own bile since roll call this morning, yes, sir."

Torin returned the smile. "Assuming that to be the case, have him send all his slowest and stupidest guards here, and reassign all the fast smart ones to double their foot patrols. Half the population of Dragon is gathered outside, and most of the remaining half will get it into their heads to take advantage of it."

"Will do, sir."

Danthres saw the sense in Torin's request, though not in his making it—it wasn't their duty to do Dragon's job for them, after all—and was about to say so when a deep voice came from behind the front desk.

"Ah, Lieutenants ban Wyvald and Tresyllione. It is well to be both of you seeing."

Turning, Danthres saw a short man with a large mustache: Olaf, the Dog and Duck's owner. Danthres had first met him fifteen years earlier, when she first showed up in Cliff's End.

Most people who came to the port city either had someplace else to go or nowhere else to go. Danthres had most assuredly been in the latter category, so when she arrived, she had stayed here until she secured a more permanent dwelling. The Dog and Duck had been the first lodgings she found in town that she could afford but did not smell like someone had died in them.

Olaf had changed very little in the intervening decade and a half. His head was still bereft of hair, save for the massive thatch between his nose and upper lip—indeed, the only significant physical change from fifteen years ago was that the huge mustache had gone from black to white. As he came out from behind the desk, Danthres had to blink from the glare of the sun shining through the windows on the staircase and reflecting off his pate. His bald head combined with his narrow shoulders, protuberant belly, and skinny legs to give him the air of a small egg balanced on a large egg balanced on two sticks.

Olaf was a native of the islands to the east, and his grasp of Common hadn't improved in fifteen years either, though Danthres suspected that it was an affectation on his part and, if pressed, he could speak the language as well as anyone in the Lord and Lady's court.

"I'm surprised to see you in such a good mood," Torin said, "given the circumstances."

"The circumstances, she is wonderful," Olaf said,

a grin trying to peek out from under his voluminous mustache. "Two years ago, I say to myself, 'Olaf,' I say, 'remodel, you need to do.' New mattresses, new curtains, new furnishings, better kitchen, new sign—even I am hiring a musician to play bar nights. All is good, close inn for month in winter when nobody come anyhow. I think this will be good, come in droves, will the people. So I close, and three more inns, they open and my business they steal! Last year been awful, but now—now it is good. 'Come to the Dog and Duck,' they will say, 'the final place resting of Gan Brightblade.' So you tell Olaf what to do, and do it, I will. I have gold mine here. Perhaps platinum mine, even."

"I'm thrilled for you," Danthres said with as little sincerity as she could muster. "What room is Brightblade in?"

"Room 12, right at stairs of the top."

"Good." She looked around for Jared, but he was probably still upstairs rousting patrons. Another guard stood at the entrance to the dining area. "You—has someone called the M.E.?"

The guard blinked several times. "I think so, ma'am."

"Someone did," Olaf said. "Came by did one of those mage-birds with message that magical examiner would arrive in an hour and a half."

"When was this?" Torin asked.

"Half an hour ago." Olaf frowned. "Why so long does it take? He is wizard, yes?"

"Yes, but a Teleportation Spell takes a great deal out of him," Torin said, "and doesn't allow him the energy to do the peel-back."

"Still," Olaf said, "so long it should not take to be walking from castle, no."

Torin grinned. "How long it takes Boneen to arrive somewhere generally has little to do with travel time and more to do with his mood. Anything over an hour usually means we woke him from a nap."

Danthres shook her head. The M.E. was a mage on loan to the Guard from the Brotherhood of Wizards, and Danthres long suspected that the cantankerous old bastard got the assignment as much to get him off the Brotherhood's own hands as anything. "An hour and a half means he was in the middle of an especially nice dream. I see no good reason to wait for him. I want to check the room before we start questioning people. Olaf, if you could wait down here—we'll want to talk to you after we've looked at the scene."

"Of course, Lieutenant Tresyllione. If you need anything, to Olaf you will come."

Shaking her head with amusement, Danthres headed upstairs. She noted that the stairs did not creak as much as they had when she'd been here before, a characteristic she attributed to Olaf's renovations. She could see why he would be irritated at the downturn in business following such extensive work, and why he would view the death of some grand hero as a good thing—especially given the crowds outside. If nothing else, the bar would probably be the hot spot of Dragon's nightlife for at least a few months. *Which means we're going to be looking into a lot of bar brawls here for the next year.*

Another guard from Dragon stood outside the room, and gave the lieutenants a respectful bow before opening the door for them.

Olaf's renovations were especially obvious in the room. Three years ago, the mattresses had been no thicker than a wafer, with modest pillows; the curtains had been burlap; and both the water basin and the desk were cheap balsa. Now, though, the mattress was far fluffier, the curtains were linen, and the basin was metal. The desk, Danthres noted, was still balsa, but it had been varnished to look like oak, and she was willing to bet that someone with less acute eyesight than hers wouldn't be able to tell the difference.

Something about the room bothered her, though.

Lying on a patch of floor between the bed and the desk was the large body of a human, half-dressed—a mail hauberk and cotton tunic lay on the bed in a heap, along with a very large sword. Armor, shirt, and weapon all looked to have been dropped on the bed by someone in the process of getting undressed. Danthres assumed the body to be that of Gan Brightblade.

"Have to admit," Torin said, "this was not how I expected Brightblade to go." He laughed. "This will play merry hell with bards across Flingaria. After all, people like Gan Brightblade don't die of broken necks in their lodgings, they die on the battlefield, valiantly saving the world from evil wizards or goblin hordes or the like."

"Goblins don't travel in hordes," Danthres said.

Torin shrugged, conceding the point. "But if they did, he'd be at the forefront of those trying to stop them."

Danthres looked over at the guard who let them in—an older foot soldier with gray-and-white stubble. Standing a post unshaven was technically against regulations, but that sort of grooming nonsense was usually only seriously enforced in Unicorn, and in headquarters when Osric was in a bad mood. "The cleaning woman found him like this?"

"Aye, ma'am," the guard said. "She came in with her key, ma'am. She be down in the kitchen, ma'am. Shall I fetch her, ma'am?"

"No, not yet."

"If she came in with the key, it means the killer locked the door," Torin said.

"Not necessarily. She probably would have assumed the door to be locked and gone for the key without even trying the handle." Danthres peered around the room. "Maybe he fell down? Tripped?"

Torin snorted. "Gan Brightblade has been called many things, but clumsy isn't one of them."

Pointing at the top of the body's head—specifically the gray hair at his temples—Danthres said, "He's not as young as he was."

"Perhaps, but the angle's all wrong—of both the body *and* the neck. For his head to have snapped that way, he'd have had to have fallen against something on his right, but the only thing on his right is empty air."

Danthres looked over at the desk. Balsa was still generally hard enough to break a neck, even as thick a one as Brightblade's. But Torin was right, in that he would never have fallen down to the floor from there into the position in which he now lay. Assuming the scene hadn't been disturbed, in any event.

Then, finally, what had been bothering her burbled to the surface. "The room smells wrong."

"He hasn't been dead long enough," Torin said.

Shaking her head, Danthres said, "Not that. It smells too—too clean."

Torin laughed. "That's Brightblade. Any other soldier, you'd expect the smells of the earth, but Brightblade was famous for bathing and grooming almost daily. I seem to recall the captain complaining about it more than once—it made the other soldiers look bad."

Danthres nodded absently. She smelled some kind of polish coming from the direction of the bed, and realized that it was from the armor that Brightblade had removed. *He polished his mail. Amazing.*

"Something's wrong here," Torin said.

"Something *else,* you mean," Danthres put in with a snort.

"Brightblade wasn't the type to go down without a fight. If he *was* killed, it was by someone who caught him completely unawares. Otherwise, he wouldn't be half-dressed with his sword on the bed. Which means it was probably someone he knew and trusted."

Danthres got down on her knees in order to get a better look at Brightblade's neck. "Look at that."

Torin did likewise on the other side of the body from her. "What am I looking at?"

"His neck."

Grinning, Torin said, "That much I determined on my own."

"No finger marks. His neck wasn't broken by hand."

"Which brings us back to him falling over—which doesn't work. Unless, of course—"

"Don't even *think* it." Danthres sighed and got back up. "I *hate* magic. And the last thing I want is the Brotherhood taking over the case. They'll make a complete troll's ear out of it, and then blame *us* when they can't solve it. That's the last thing we need right now."

Nodding sagely, Torin said, "Agreed. Brightblade had dinner at the castle with the Lord and Lady many times—Osric was an old friend of his. They'll both want this one closed quickly and efficiently, and neither one will want the Brotherhood involved."

"Not that they'll have a choice if he died by magical means." Danthres snarled.

Torin spoke in as grave a voice as Danthres had ever heard the usually jovial lieutenant use. "We need to take this one slowly and carefully. Even if there is no magic, Osric and the Lord and Lady will be breathing down our necks."

Danthres shook her head. "I've never even heard of this idiot before today, and he's already giving me a headache. Boneen'll handle the peel-back if he ever deigns to arrive and we can take it from there." One of the M.E.'s main functions—and the main reason why Danthres was willing to put up with having to deal with a mage on a daily basis—was to cast an Inanimate Residue Spell. Everyone called it a "peel-back" because it could, according to the explanation Boneen's predecessor had given Danthres when she first signed up for the Guard, "read the psychic resonances on inanimate objects." Translated into Common, it showed the spellcaster what happened to those objects in the recent past. This was handy when investigating a crime. "Meantime, let's talk to who we need to talk to." To the guard, she said, "Don't let anyone other than Lieutenant ban Wyvald, myself, or the M.E. in here, am I understood?"

"Aye, ma'am."

Olaf gave them the use of a storage room in which to question witnesses. Danthres found it adequate, though not as well suited to the task as the interview rooms back at the castle. Too bad that transporting everyone they needed to talk to back there was impractical.

The first person they spoke to was the cleaning woman who found the body. Her cheeks were still puffy from crying, she broke into sobs every third sentence, and she would periodically ask what kind of world they lived in when great heroes like Gan Brightblade died, but eventually Danthres, with Torin's help, was able to get out of her that she went to Room 12 first in the hopes of getting a look at Brightblade, opened the locked door with her key—yes, she was sure it was locked, the door clicked when she put in the skeleton key—and entered to find the body on the floor. Torin asked if she knocked first, and, blushing, the woman admitted that she didn't, hoping to catch Brightblade in some kind of state of undress. That was followed by another sobbing jag and yet another query as to the kind of world they lived in. Once they got past that again, the woman said that she just stood in the threshold screaming for who-knew-how-long, until one of the other cleaning women took her down to the kitchen.

Another cleaning woman verified her account, saying that she didn't move from the threshold for almost a full minute, " 'fore I was able to be gettin' her ass down the stairs" while Olaf called the Guard. That cleaning woman also pointed out that Brightblade's corpse seemed to have more lines on his face and more gray hair than he had had the night before, though she allowed as how that might have simply been the difference between seeing him in sunlight, as opposed to the dimmer illumination of the previous evening.

Talking to Olaf confirmed Danthres's worst fears: Brightblade had checked in the previous morning alongside an elf, a dwarf, a human priest, a barbarian from the north ("I had to be giving him the room in the far corner so stink my inn he doesn't") and two halflings.

Torin looked at Danthres. "Our heroic quest."

Olaf shrugged. "I do not know if they are questing, but I do know that they acted like old friends. Dinner they had together, yes, and laugh a lot they did. They even handle gawkers with goodness. Ate and drank, they did, all the night long."

Danthres looked at Torin. "We're going to need to talk to them."

The time-chimes sounded ten, and Boneen still hadn't shown up, even though it was now two hours since he sent the mage-bird. ("It must have been a particularly good dream," Torin commented.) Torin suggested that they split the interviews with the rest of Brightblade's party. Olaf gave Torin use of the kitchen, leaving Danthres to remain in the storage room. Since elves tended to view half-breeds as inferiors beneath their notice, dwarves generally hated anyone with any elven blood, and Danthres had the more sensitive nose, Torin took the elf, dwarf, and barbarian, leaving Danthres with the priest and the two halflings.

She decided to take the priest first. The man who entered the storage room introduced himself in a soft voice as Brother Genero of Velessa. Having spent some time in Treemark, which had the highest concentration of Temisans in Flingaria, Danthres recognized Genero instantly as a priest of that goddess. He wore the trademark bright red robe, had grown the traditional long, braided chin-beard (but no mustache), and had shaved his head aside from one circle of hair on the crown, tied into a topknot. The robe was ankle-length, and quite battered. It looked to her like it hadn't been cleaned in over a month—which tracked with the travel time from Velessa to Cliff's End on horseback. Under the robes, Danthres could see leather armor, which surprised her. She also noted that he walked with his hand angled at his left hip, as if he was expecting a scabbard to be there. This meant he often traveled armed and that he was right-handed.

An armed and armored priest. Interesting.

As he sat down on one of Olaf's wobbly wooden chairs, Genero offered the blessings of Temisa on the Cliff's End Castle Guard, to which Danthres grunted indifferently. Although both sides of her heritage had numerous religious traditions, Danthres had not been raised in any of them during her childhood in Sorlin; that sort of thing didn't go on there, particularly when she was a girl. What she'd seen since departing that place—both before and after getting involved with law enforcement in Cliff's End—led her to think that the gods were capricious at best.

"It's such a tragic waste," Genero said, looking down at the floor. "I have to admit, I never thought that Gan would go on to greet the next life in this way. I expected him to die in a fight—or failing that, as an old man in bed surrounded by beautiful women. Perhaps Temisa has rewarded him with that in the afterlife."

"Perhaps," Danthres said dryly, wondering if *everyone* was going to comment on the unexpectedness of Brightblade's mode of dying, "but I'm more concerned with how he got there."

Genero looked over at the wall. "I'm sure it was just an accident. He'd been drinking quite a bit, and he could be a very clumsy drunk."

"So you don't think he was murdered?"

"No, of course not." He peered up at the ceiling. "Gan was one of the great heroes of our time."

"They tend to be the ones with the longest list of enemies."

Now, finally, Genero looked at Danthres. "I can assure you, Lieutenant, that all of Gan's enemies are quite dead."

"Really?" Danthres asked dubiously. "How lucky for him." She leaned back in her own chair. "I'm told, Brother, that you and Mr. Brightblade arrived here along with five others. What was your business in Cliff's End?"

"We were on our way to hire a boat. In fact, Gan and I planned to go to the Docklands to begin the hiring process this morning." He smiled slightly, the first time his facial expression had truly changed since he walked in. "Obviously, that will have to be postponed."

"Obviously," Danthres said, making a mental note to send a message to Mermaid Precinct to have their foot patrols keep an eye out on the Docklands for the remaining six members of this little group. If any of them made any move to hire a boat, she and Torin needed to know about it. "Where were you headed?"

"No place in particular." Genero again looked at the wall. "We were simply looking to take a voyage onto the Garamin Sea and enjoy ourselves."

It was everything Danthres could do to keep from laughing out loud. "A 'voyage'?"

"Yes."

"Just to some random destination on the Garamin?"

Again, Genero looked at Danthres. "You seem to have trouble believing me."

You don't know the half of it. "Look at it from my perspective, Brother—the idea that an elf and a dwarf would take a pleasure cruise together is a difficult one for me to wrap my mind around. Add in that they're taking it with three humans and two halflings, and I'm afraid I find it impossible to believe that it's just for pleasure."

Genero nodded. "I can see why you in particular would think that, given your background."

Danthres's mood soured even further. But then, her dual heritage was fairly obvious. Her face combined the worst elements of the two races: her mother's wide nose, large brown eyes, and shallow cheekbones did not go at all with her father's pointed ears, high forehead, or thin lips.

"I'm sorry," Genero said quickly, "I didn't mean to give offense."

Favoring the priest with her nastiest smile, Danthres said, "When you've given me offense, Brother, you won't have any trouble knowing it."

"No doubt. I assume, based on your age and accent, that your parents' union was not a happy one?"

Danthres's first rule of interrogation was that she asked all the questions; besides which, she had no interest in discussing her life with a murder suspect. "I don't see how that's relevant, Brother."

"My point is that you'd naturally be suspicious of an elf willingly traveling with a human and a dwarf. And understandably so. But we have been through much, the seven of us. Today, Lieutenant, you live in a Flingaria that is at peace. For decades, that was not the case—human warred on human, elf warred on human, western elf warred on eastern elf, dwarf warred on elf, trolls warred on just about everyone—not to mention crazed wizards like Chalmraik or Mitos. But now, the human lands are united, the western elves are no more, and the elves and dwarves have a treaty. The plague of megalomaniacal wizards has ended." He pointed to the doorway that led to the rest of the inn. "My comrades and I were at the forefront of much of that. It is in part through our efforts that there is such peace now. Through those hardships we have formed a bond, and we simply wish to enjoy the fruits of our labors."

It was a very pretty speech, both heartfelt and convincing. Genero gave it with all the conviction one would expect of a man who had dedicated his life to the service of one of the gods, and Danthres didn't believe a word of it.

She asked several more questions, most relating to where Genero was last night and this morning, but they were secondary. Her main question had been answered virtually the moment Genero had walked into the storage room.

Brother Genero of Velessa and his group had a very specific purpose in mind, and Danthres was fairly sure that the priest knew—or at least thought he knew—precisely who murdered Gan Brightblade.

The questioning of the two halflings—twins named Mari and Nari—went about as Danthres expected. They told the same sea-cruise lie as Genero, with just enough variations in their stories to sound convincingly unrehearsed, which made it all the more obvious that they'd gotten their stories straight ahead of time. Cliff's End had more than its share of grifters, and Danthres suspected that these two would fit right in on Jorbin's Way. Danthres patiently asked them most of the same questions she'd given the priest, and they responded with multiple digressions, numerous evasions, and a general refusal to give anything like a straight answer.

When she was done with Nari, Danthres went back to the lobby, where Torin was already waiting. "Boneen finally put in his appearance about a quarter of an hour ago," he said. "The peel-back should be finished shortly." The spell took about half an hour and required that there be nothing living besides the spellcaster present.

"Good." Danthres peered up the stairs to see that the gray-and-white-stubbled guard was back to standing outside Room 12. Then she filled Torin in on her interviews. "What about yours?"

"The elf was Olthar lothSirhans."

"Another celebrity."

Torin grunted. "Well, this particular war hero was close-mouthed, arrogant, and gave one-word answers. That interview took only a few minutes and he couldn't get out of the kitchen fast enough when I said we were done. Ubàrlig, the dwarf, was considerably more voluble, especially once he found out we work for Osric. It turns out he and the captain met several years back. He acted very open and friendly—but he didn't give me any more than lothSirhans."

"Let me guess—we're all old friends going on a cruise through the Garamin."

Torin nodded. "Mind you, he was carrying his axe with him—a Fjorm."

Danthres blinked. "He has a Fjorm?"

"Yes. One of only six left—I even asked him about it, and he was more than happy to talk about how he got it and how many elves he killed with it, all without getting a scratch on the blade."

"It must be worth a fortune." Danthres snorted. "I'm amazed those two halflings haven't tried to steal it."

Torin grinned. "Perhaps they have." The grin fell. "In any event, one doesn't take such an item onto a pleasure cruise—especially if one is a dwarven general of Ubàrlig's reputation. If he's brought that axe, he intends to use it."

"So whatever heroic quest these idiots were going on, it's been derailed. We need to find out what it was."

"I spoke to a few of the patrons who were sitting next to our merry band last night. Apprently, Brightblade, Ubàrlig, lothSirhans, and Bogg spent most of the night telling stories of their assorted campaigns, conquests, battles, and triumphs—and," he added with a grin, "that was just their sexual exploits. Speaking of which, I can't imagine that any of Bogg's—that's our barbarian—were with a woman who had a nose. I'm quite sure his skin has never known the touch of soap, and I'd be willing to bet several silvers that it hasn't even encountered water that wasn't rain. He spent most of the interview talking about how he would cut off the head of whoever killed Brightblade and then eat it."

Before Danthres could respond to the visual image that provoked, she heard a door open from up the stairs. She looked up to see the squat form of Boneen exit the room. Dressed in a brown linen shirt that was about a size too small for him and matching pants that were a size too big, the magical examiner came down the stairs on his stubby legs, a scowl deepening his already heavily lined face. His oversized pants flapped as he came down. The pungent, spicy aroma of the spell ingredients preceded him, and Danthres could see the residue of same on his hands.

"What is it about you two?" he asked without preamble. "You always get the cases that give me heartburn."

Danthres felt her stomach flutter. "What do you mean? What did the spell tell you?"

"Not a damn thing! The victim was just standing in the room when his neck broke and he fell to the floor."

Torin blinked. "He can't possibly have broken his neck when he fell down. The angle—"

"Please, ban Wyvald, pay *attention* when I'm talking to you," Boneen snapped. "His neck broke, *then* he fell to the floor."

Now Danthres's stomach went into a full-on grind. "Magic."

"No."

This time, Danthres blinked. "What do you mean, 'no'?"

Boneen raised his eyebrows. "I assume you know what the word means. . . ."

"Very funny."

"I can assure you that I could detect no magical forces at work at all anywhere in that room."

Danthres shook her head. "How can someone's neck just break like that without magic being involved?"

Folding his arms, Boneen said, "That, Tresyllione, is an excellent question. I, for one, am grateful that answering it is not my problem, but rather yours, since this is your case. Best of luck to you. Now, if you'll excuse me, I'm going back to the castle and finishing the nap that was so rudely interrupted for this exercise in futility."

With that, the M.E. turned and stalked out of the inn—as much as a several-hundred-year-old wizard with short stubby legs wearing oversized pants *could* stalk.

When he opened the door, Danthres noted that the crowd had thinned out considerably, down to only a dozen or so stragglers.

"It could still be magic," Torin said. "Remember, some priests have a modicum of magical ability."

"A very small modicum," Danthres said. The Brotherhood, in their infinite generosity, permitted some priests to manipulate magic to a slight degree, a stipulation that Danthres chalked up to the political expediency of not pissing off people who had direct lines to the assorted pantheons of gods. Of course, as she had seen, Genero was hardly an ordinary priest, either. "Anyhow, I doubt Boneen would miss that. Even when he's being this peevish, he takes pride in his work."

"True." Torin sighed. "We've been proceeding on the assumption that Brightblade was killed by someone he knew. What if it was someone he knew who wasn't even in the room?"

Danthres rubbed the bridge of her nose between her index finger and thumb. "We've been at this all day. Let's have graybeard up there get a detail together to remove the body and let Olaf have his inn back." She looked up the stairs at the now-open door to Room 12. "This better not be magic. I *hate* magic."

Two

The smell of dead fish, salt water, and sweat combined to cheer Horran as he walked along the Docklands of Cliff's End. For the first time in years, he was back on day patrol.

He strolled down the northernmost part of the dock, nodding to the shipmasters and dockworkers he knew—which was most of them—and observing the loading of crates, the off-loading of more crates, the casting off of fishing boats, the arguing over payments, and the embarkation of passengers. More than one commented on his now being on the day shift.

"So," Abo, the first mate of the *Breeze,* asked when Horran passed by that vessel, "who'd you blow to get the cushy shift?"

"Blow, hell. Eleven years, Abo. Eleven years working

this place at night. I *earned* the damned cushy shift."

"Aw, c'mon, Horran, you're gonna miss breakin' up brawls at the Dancing Seagull."

"Yes, because I live to stop drunken sailors from pounding other drunken sailors."

"Careful with that thing!" Abo yelled at one of his sailors, who was struggling with a crate. "Drop that, and it's garnished from your wages."

"You don't pay your sailors enough to garnish anything."

Abo grinned. "That's their problem. Anyhow, *I'm* gonna miss you breakin' up brawls at the Seagull. You're the one who pried that gnome off my ass last year. Couldn't sit for a week."

"When do you get to sit?"

The grin widened. "At the Seagull when I drink."

"Well, tonight, the drinks're on me, because the only reason I'm going into that place now is to hoist one *after* my shift, not arrest a third of the sailors on this damn dock for drunk and disorderly, another third for assault and battery, and the rest of you for graft and trafficking of illegal goods. Now I can just watch you load and unload, feel the sun on my face, smell the day's catches come noontime, and actually sleep at night."

"Bet you five coppers you're bored shitless in a month."

Horran couldn't imagine that happening—but then it was only his first day. Still and all, he said, "It's a bet."

After he and Abo shook on it, he noticed a sound that was completely out of place.

Abo apparently noticed it, too. "What the hell's that?"

The guard's eyes widened. "That's plate armor. Some idiot's walking around in full plate armor." He put a gloved hand on Abo's shoulder. "This I *need* to check out. Catch you at the Seagull tonight?"

"Drinks're really on you? Damn right, I'll be there." Abo turned back to see that the sailor was stumbling again. "Dammit, what did I just tell you?"

Chuckling, Horran moved toward the distinctive clanking of armor on wood, which seemed to be coming from the vicinity of where the *Esmerelda* was docked. He couldn't believe anyone was that stupid. While a full suit of armor was very useful if you were riding a horse to face your enemy on an open field, on the open sea it would serve only to guarantee that you would sink to the bottom and drown if you fell overboard.

Sure enough, a good-sized man wearing plate armor was approaching the gangplank that led to the *Esmerelda*. "Ho, Captain Zaile! I am prepared to depart!" The *Esmerelda* was primarily a cargo ship that covered the assorted islands on the Garamin, but Horran knew that the ship's master, Zaile, would sometimes take on a passenger or two if he had a light load.

Zaile himself, a stooped old man with a thick gray beard and thicker gray hair, came down the gangplank to meet the armored fellow. "That's what you're wearing, eh?"

"Of course. If I am to slay Chalmraik the Foul, then I must needs protect myself." The man's voice echoed slightly, reverberating through his armor. Horran noted that he had a huge sword on a belt scabbard and a pack on his back. The guard suspected that this man had aspirations of being the next Gan Brightblade. Based on the whispers he'd been hearing since coming on this morning, that position was apparently open.

"If you insist," Zaile said, "but I'm afraid I'll have to be raisin' your fare, then. Extra weight, you understand."

"How much?" The would-be wizard-slayer sounded unconcerned.

"Two gold."

"Done," he said without hesitation.

It took all of Horran's self-control not to laugh out loud. One gold was exorbitant for the meagre accommodations on the *Esmerelda,* and the added weight of one suit of armor was a pittance compared with the weight of any cargo that would normally be taking up the space Zaile was giving to this idiot.

"Oh, and there'll be another passenger to share the quarters with. I believe he has the same destination as you."

"What?"

"Captain Zaile," Horran said, approaching this tableau.

Squinting in annoyance, Zaile said, "Horran. Didn't know you were on day shift."

"Yeah, the bosses decided to thank me for keeping old sea-bitches like you honest."

"What are you saying, my good sir?" the man in the armor asked. "Captain Zaile is as honest as they come. I have it on good authority from many sources."

Most of whom are getting a piece of that two gold in exchange for the testimonial, Horran thought. "Oh, Zaile's reputation precedes him, that's for damn sure. If you'll excuse me, uh—"

The armored man moved to an at-attention stance that bespoke some past military service. "I am Kaylin the Mighty. Word has reached me that Chalmraik the Foul is alive and well and plotting to take over Flingaria once more."

"Really?" Horran asked dryly.

Gravely, Kaylin spoke with the tone of one over whose head Horran's sarcasm had sailed. "Indeed it has. But worry not. I have obtained a sword—" he patted his scabbard with a gauntleted hand "—that is blessed with the Runes of Tyrac."

Again, Horran resisted the urge to laugh out loud. "That's wonderful. Kaylin, I need to speak with Captain Zaile in private, just for a second. Don't worry," he added quickly, "it won't have any impact on what I'm sure's a real noble quest." He turned to the captain and indicated a section of dock near the *Esmerelda*'s aft section. "Zaile?"

As soon as they were out of Kaylin's earshot, Zaile said, "Don't you be ruinin' this'un for me, Horran! This idjit's a blessed gold mine!"

Horran smiled. "Last time I checked, Zaile, the extortion laws don't take into account how idiotic the mark is."

"Oh for Wiate's sake, he ain't just idiotic, he's downright stupid. Practically catatonic, even. He's wearin' armor on a boat. He thinks Chalmraik is still alive. He fell for the 'Runes of Tyrac' scam, for Wiate's sake! I didn't think anyone still be *usin'* that one, much less fallin' for it."

"Damn. You must feel strong about this guy—you invoked Wiate twice in one conversation," Horran said with a smile.

Pointing one crooked, bony finger at Horran, Zaile said, "Don't you be sassin' me, boy. I remember when you were just a little demon tryin' to steal fish outta my nets with that brother'a yours. Hell, I remember when the Guard first arrested you. Shoulda sent you down the hole 'stead'a rewardin' you."

Horran's jaw torqued in annoyance. He'd grown up in the Docklands an orphan, first supported by his older brother—one of the Docklands' more talented thieves—then on his own after his brother was killed. Unfortunately, Horran was not as talented as his sibling, and was caught by the Castle Guard, who gave him a choice: jail time, or serving as an errand boy for the Guard. Since he wasn't stupid, and he knew what jail was like for young boys, Horran chose the latter.

Eventually, he joined the Guard formally, and lasted eleven years as exactly the kind of guard he and his brother used to evade as kids.

Zaile was still wagging his finger. "I'll not be stopped from makin' a livin' by the likes'a you."

"Hey, you wanna make a living, Zaile, that's fine with me, but takin' advantage of someone this brain-dead is not only illegal, it's *cruel*. I mean, come on, would you overcharge a legless man for a wheelchair?"

Zaile let out a long-suffering sigh. "How much?"

Horran smiled. *Took him long enough.* "Two silvers—one for each gold piece you're charging Kaylin the Moron." He was going to charge him only one silver, but Zaile had to go and bring up Horran's misspent youth. Besides, he needed the cash. While his salary paid for food and lodging, it was the hundreds of bribes he'd taken over the past decade that he really needed. Four years hence, when he got his fifteen-year bonus and then retired, those bribes would combine with the bonus to buy a house in Dragon or even possibly Unicorn, and allow him to live out life in luxury.

Or at least more luxury than a failed orphan sneak-thief could have possibly dreamed of as a boy . . .

"Done." Zaile shook his head. "Shoulda just been sayin' so in the first place. Saved me all'a this trouble." Zaile reached into his money pouch and pulled out a silver piece. " 'Sall I got on me right now. I'm bein' good for the other half."

"Oh, I'm *sure* you are." Horran grinned. "Captain Zaile is as honest as they come. I have it on good authority from many sources."

"Very funny."

"How *darest* thou!?"

Horran whirled around to see that someone else—wearing mail and also carrying a very large sword—had spoken those words to Kaylin. His pattern of speech indicated that he had learned Common in the far lands to the west where they still insisted on the archaic forms.

"How dare *I?*" Kaylin replied, sounding outraged. "I have been chosen by the Runes of Tyrac to be the one, the only true warrior who shall slay Chalmraik the Foul! It has been written."

As he ran over to break up the potential altercation, Horran thought, *Whoever ran the Tyrac scam on Kaylin really laid it on thick.*

"Thou worm! Thou varlet! Thou hobgoblin! 'Twas *I* the gods chose to slay the evil wizard, and thou shalt not take my birthright from me!" The newcomer unsheathed his own broadsword.

Horran shook his head. The blade had been inscribed with the so-called Runes of Tyrac—in truth it was gibberish using letters from the old Pohldak script that, according to one of Horran's old sergeants, loosely translated to "all flips harried elk."

"None shall deny Erik ban Soreyl from the destiny that be rightfully his! Have at thee!"

Standing between them, putting one hand on the chest of each man, Horran said, "*One's* gonna deny you. Put your sword away, sir."

Not taking his eyes—which, Horran noticed, were coal black—off of Kaylin, ban Soreyl said, "Stand aside, good sir. Whilst I have no wish to harm thee, no man shall come between me and my one true destiny."

"If you don't put your sword away, Mr. ban Soreyl, your only destiny's gonna be to spend the night in the hole." The holding cells in the precincts weren't actually holes, but that nickname was given to the dungeons beneath the castle where criminals were held, and, when the Lord and Lady established the Castle Guard and the separate precincts, the holding cells in the precinct houses were given the same appellation.

Kaylin chose that moment to speak up. "This fool speaks true, good sir Guard. Allow us to settle this as men."

Horran caught the eye of one of the youth squad in the quickly gathering crowd—nothing the populace liked better than to watch a good brawl, especially in the Docklands—and gave him an eye-signal that indicated that he needed help. The boy nodded and ran off to find more guards on foot patrol and bring them to the *Esmerelda*. *Gotta remember to give him a copper later*, he thought, though the boy himself would no doubt provide a reminder when this was all over. Certainly Horran himself never forgot to bill the guards he helped out.

Then he turned to Kaylin, whose hand was on his scabbard. "I'm afraid I can't let you to do that."

"Nonsense," Kaylin said, now pulling out his sword. "Laws are for lesser men, not heroes such as us."

"I don't give a troll's ass if you're Gan Brightblade his own self, if you don't put those swords away, I'll bring both of you in."

"Hah!" ban Soreyl said, his gaze now falling on Kaylin's blade, which also discussed the acrobatic habits of beleaguered elk. "I see some fool has tricked thy gullible self into purchasing a sword with false runes. It shall be my greatest privilege to rid the world of such a fool as thee."

"Nobody's ridding nobody of nothing!"

Everything happened very quickly after that. Ban Soreyl lunged with his sword. Horran tried to hold him back. Kaylin raised his own sword, but then lost his balance—apparently not taking the extra weight of his plate armor into account—and fell backward onto the dock. Then ban Soreyl stumbled, his own target having disappeared and Horran's attempt to restrain him throwing *his* balance off, and both guard and swordsman fell to the dock in a heap.

Horran spent two seconds lying on the dock listening to the whoops, cheers, and laughter—mostly the latter—of the crowd before rolling out from under the squirming form of ban Soreyl. Both would-be heroes seemed to be having difficulty with the seemingly simple action of getting up while wearing armor. Horran smiled as he got to his feet. *The bards don't usually include the part about how hard it is to get up off the ground in that stuff, do they?*

When Horran first joined up, he was on day shift, because that's where you started. Putting rookies on night shift in Mermaid was tantamount to a death sentence. In the two years he spent there before being "promoted" to night duty, Horran had never drawn his sword. In fact, most guards went through their entire careers without ever using their swords, and only those assigned to Goblin and to night patrol in Mermaid even had occasion to draw them. So it was with a particular irritation that Horran drew his right now, even as he heard the distinctive booted footfalls of his fellow day-patrol guards coming to his aid.

"When you two manage to get up off your asses, you're both coming with me." More formally, he said: "In the name of Lord Albin and Lady Meerka, I hereby place you, Erik ban Soreyl, and you, Kaylin the Mo—the Mighty"—he almost said "the Moron" again—"under arrest for assault on a member of the Cliff's End Castle Guard and for creating a public disturbance. Other charges to be added as necessary."

Then he sighed. Those words had changed a day

that should have been simple and easy into a mess of paperwork, tiresome interrogations, endless digressions, and more dealing with Zaile, who would be very aggravated at losing two passengers—and probably not give Horran the other silver he owed him.

Day patrol was supposed to be less *exciting, dammit.*

Three

Captain Osric was sharpening his dagger on a battered old stone as Torin and Danthres entered his office. The time-chimes had rung eighteen only a few minutes before, meaning it was less than an hour before the day shift came to an end. Under his beard, Torin frowned. Osric sharpened his dagger only when he had bad news to impart. If he was already honing the damn thing before they'd even come into the room, the news had to be dire.

Torin owed much to the captain. They had fought side by side years earlier when Osric was a well-regarded troop commander and Torin was an eager young idiot who left the semi-isolated city-state of Myverin to seek his fortune as a soldier. When Osric lost an eye in battle, he came to Cliff's End and gladly took on an administrative post overseeing the Castle Guard. When Torin heard this, he too came to Cliff's End, grateful for the opportunity to work with his old friend again, and finding satisfaction as a detective. He'd left Myverin because his family's near-utopian existence as philosophers there bored him to tears; he'd lost interest in soldiering because the lack of intellectual stimulation did likewise. Serving as one of Osric's lieutenants, he was able to combine both into a satisfying whole.

As Torin and Danthres each took a seat in the guest chairs opposite Osric, the captain's usual scowl was deep enough to virtually etch a crater into his perpetually unshaven face. Both lieutenants knew that he deliberately kept his beard at a length that looked like a day's growth—Danthres's sensitive nose picked up the shaving lotion he used—but that didn't change the visual effect it had, combined with the black silk patch over his left eye.

"I've spent most of the afternoon talking with Lord Albin. He is *very* upset, as you might imagine."

"We know what you're going to say, Captain," Torin said quickly. "Gan Brightblade is a hero renowned throughout Flingaria, he is a dear friend of Lord Albin and Lady Meerka, and we need to close this case with all due speed and dispatch."

Osric continued to sharpen his dagger. "Very perceptive. I just got back, so I haven't had the chance to talk to Boneen. What did the peel-back say?"

"Nothing," Danthres said.

"What do you mean, 'nothing'?"

Torin shrugged. "Just what she said. According to

Boneen, Brightblade's neck broke, then he fell to the floor. And no magic was involved whatsoever."

"How is that possible?"

"You tell me," Danthres said, blowing out a breath. "We've been talking about it all day, but we've got nothing."

"I don't want to hear that." Osric scraped his dagger against the sharpening stone so hard it made Torin's teeth rattle. He shuddered to think what effect it was having on Danthres. "This is the biggest murder we've ever seen. People are going to wonder what the point is of a castle guard if we can't even keep a hero like Gan Brightblade safe. They may start to think we're better off with a formal militia or a standing army to keep things safe. They'll also think that the captain and lieutenants should be replaced. So kindly don't tell me you have nothing."

Torin was thinking that Osric's dagger had never been sharper even as he spoke. "The only thing we do have is the rest of his group."

"What group?"

Quickly, Torin filled the captain in on Genero and the rest of the party. "They obviously came here for some other reason than a pleasure cruise."

"Genero knows who killed Brightblade," Danthres added, "or at least he thinks he does."

"They all do."

Osric finally put the sharpening stone down. "I remember Ubàrlig. You sure he's lying?"

"Through what few teeth he has left," Torin said. "He brought a Fjorm axe with him."

Now Osric started tapping his desk with the dagger. "You're right, if he brought the Fjorm, he's going into combat. Dammit."

"Genero said they'd been through a great deal together," Danthres said. "They've fought wizards, warlords, what-have-you. One of them might've picked something up, something Boneen couldn't detect, and used it on Brightblade."

"What about the patrons?"

Torin shrugged. "The usual you find at the Dog and Duck. Transients, people on their way out to sea, people on their way back home from the sea. Most were only staying the one night. Only long-termer was a young man who said he was waiting to meet some members of his family here on the way to a wedding in Iaron next spring. None of them seemed to have the wherewithal to do something on this scale. Even so, we've asked all of them to extend their stays, and they're all willing." Torin grinned. "They all wish to cooperate with the investigation of the murder of so great a hero."

Danthres snorted. "Right, so they can tell their friends that they helped the Guard find the man who killed Gan Brightblade."

Osric leaned back in his chair. "I've been to dozens of spring weddings in Iaron, Tresyllione—trust me, that's the kind of story that can only lighten it up."

"I'll take your word for it. I have no plans to ever set foot in Iaron."

The captain put the dagger down, finally. "I want this case closed. I can give you extra help if you want it."

"Not the idiots on the other shift, please," Danthres said in a pleading voice.

"That's all I've got. I can't take the others off their cases."

"I don't *want* Dru and Hawk off their case," Danthres said. "That damn rapist needs to be taken down."

"Agreed," Torin said, "though that only leaves Iaian and Grovis."

The look on Danthres's face made it clear what she thought of that notion. Torin had to suppress a grin. Iaian was long past it, and Grovis was never in any danger of approaching it.

Osric shook his head. "Doesn't matter. If I take them off the fake-glamour ring, the Brotherhood'll cut out my other eye."

Torin grinned. "Can't Lord Albin intervene?"

"I assume that was a joke, ban Wyvald." Osric picked up the dagger again. "The only people in Flingaria who are unmoved by Gan Brightblade's death are the Brotherhood of Wizards. As far as they're concerned, there's no more important case than the bad glamours." He leaned forward again, pointing his dagger at the lieutenants. "But as far as I'm concerned, yours is. All right, since I can't give you any extra detectives, I can at least give you extra guards for foot patrols or rounding people up."

"Good," Danthres said. "We'll need Mermaid to see if any of our gang of seven tried to hire a boat. Genero said he and Brightblade were going to do that today, but I don't see any good reason to believe him."

"He's a Temisan priest, Tresyllione." Osric's incredulity was understandable to Torin. While the clergy of the dozens of religions that were favored in this part of Flingaria had its share of charlatans and ne'er-do-wells, Torin knew that those who worshiped Temisa were among the most well regarded and tended toward both the lowest amount of corruption and the nastiest punishment of same.

Danthres, however, would not be dissuaded. "He's a Temisan priest who wears a sword and leather armor and lies to investigators, Captain."

Osric nodded. "Fair point."

"And we'll need to backtrack their movements," Torin said. "Maybe they encountered someone on the way here. And we should question whoever took in their horses outside the city."

"That *we'll* do," Danthres added.

"I'll make sure Jonas takes care of you," Osric said. "What else?"

Danthres looked at Torin, then back at Osric. "We also should talk to Brightblade's friends again, but not until tomorrow after they've had time to sleep on it."

"In their rooms this time," Torin added. "I want to get a look at their accommodations."

Nodding, Danthres continued: "If one of them did it, having a night to think about what they've done might make them more nervous. After all, they're self-styled heroes, but not murderers, and first-time murderers usually have a hard time sleeping."

In fact, Torin knew that many of the murderers they'd put away in their decade together, first-time or not, had no trouble sleeping, but Torin also made it a rule never to disagree with Danthres in front of the captain. It was better that he thought they were a perfect team—just as it was better that he thought they were intimidated by his stubble and eyepatch. It made the work run more smoothly.

"All right," Osric said, sheathing the dagger. "Take all the overtime you need on this."

Torin straightened. "Really?"

Osric rarely smiled, but now his face did soften a bit. "That was the first thing I asked Lord Albin for. After all, if we are to solve the most important murder in Cliff's End's history, no resource should be spared, right?" The scowl came back. "Now get out of here and close this case."

As they exited Osric's office, Danthres shook her head and chuckled. "Amazing."

"What is?"

"Until now, I've been cursing Brightblade's name—a mystery like this is usually just a major pain in the ass until we put the case down, but unlimited overtime? For that, I will happily drink a toast to Gan Brightblade at the Chain tonight."

"Assuming we *get* to the Chain. I think it behooves us to at least question the stablemasters tonight." Torin grinned. "We *do* have unlimited overtime, after all."

It was close to midnight by the time Danthres and Torin showed up at The Old Ball and Chain—late enough, Danthres observed, that Iaian had already gone home and there were actually a few seats available.

The public house had been opened six years earlier by a retired dwarven guard named Urgoss. His fellow foot soldiers of Dragon Precinct had come to the grand opening, and kept coming back every night. Soon, the place gained a reputation as a Guard bar, to the point where Urgoss would only let non-Guard personnel in if they were specifically vouched for—sometimes not even then, depending on the quality of the person giving the reference.

Danthres spied Dru and Hawk at their usual table—the big round one in the back—and pointed Torin toward it. Urgoss had arranged the tables so that there were plenty of clear walkways to and from the bar, thus saving him the expense of hiring table service. Besides, he figured if you were too drunk to amble up to the bar and order your own drink, you shouldn't have any more anyhow. The back wall of the Chain had a long bench with five six-person tables alongside it. Hawk sat on the bench against the wall, with Dru in one of the two stools opposite.

"About time you two showin' up," Hawk said, holding up his flagon in tribute. Danthres could smell the ale both in the flagon and on Hawk's breath.

Torin grinned as he slid onto the bench next to Hawk. "The joys of unlimited overtime."

Dru's eyes went as wide as copper coins. "Osric signed off on that?"

Shrugging, Danthres took the stool next to Dru. "Well, we have to have some compensation for having him take up residence in our asses for the duration of this case."

"Good," Hawk said, "maybe he'll be gettin' outta ours, then."

"Could be worse," Dru said after taking a contemplative sip of his ale. "At least we don't have the Brotherhood up there like Iaian and the fish do." Dru had taken to referring to Grovis as "the fish" because he felt the perpetually confused look on the lieutenant's face resembled that of one of his wife's piscine pets.

"No, we just gotta listen to 'im bitch an' moan 'bout it."

Again, Torin grinned. "Ah, so we missed Iaian's usual gripe session entirely, then?"

"Yeah, he faded about an hour ago." Dru wiped the foam from his ale off his lips. "Least he isn't going on about the fish anymore."

Danthres snorted. "How many different ways can you say that Grovis is a perfect ass?"

"Iaian's come up with most of them by now, I should think," Torin said.

"Well, we missed tonight's griping by virtue of spending several hours figuring out which stable Brother Genero, Gan Brightblade, and their merry band of idiots used to house their horses when they arrived. Took forever to find—probably because we started at the cheaper places, and worked our way up."

Dru almost sputtered his ale. "You're kidding, right? Heavy hitter like Brightblade, he's gonna go with the biggest, snazziest stable he can find."

"Our logic," Torin said, "is that they're going on a sea voyage, so they'd be looking to economize on their long-term storage." Then the grin returned. "At least, that is how we will justify our mode of search when we put in the overtime request."

All four of them laughed. "Good move," Dru said. "Who knows when you'll get a shot like this again?"

"Damn straight." Danthres got up. "First round's on me."

"Try twelfth round," Hawk said, "but we'll be takin' it."

Chuckling, Danthres worked her way to the other side of the Chain, where Urgoss stood behind the wide, wooden bar. The surface was pockmarked with the nicks and scrapes of six years' worth of drunken guards' actions, including several attempts at initial-carving and amateur relief sculpture. Urgoss never bothered to fix it up, on the theory that it didn't interfere with his ability to provide drinks, so why should he bother? The dwarf himself stood on a raised platform that gave the illusion of greater height.

Three guards wearing the crest of Mermaid on their armor were nursing flagons at the bar as Danthres approached. She recognized one of them as Horran, a veteran; the other two weren't old enough to shave every day. Horran was regaling the youngsters with some tale or other.

". . . so they fall on top of each other, and I have to actually draw my weapon. They both start going on about how they can't defeat Chalmraik if I take 'em in, and Zaile starts peeing in his shorts 'cause he's out two passenger fares." Horran shook his head. "Lousy way to start back on day shift."

Urgoss saw Danthres and started to walk down his platform toward her. She held up four fingers; Urgoss stopped, nodded, and grabbed four flagons.

"They've got you back on days, Horran?" she said to the old guard.

He laughed. "Yeah, Lieutenant, starting today. Time off for bad behavior. So I get these two nutcases who think they're 'destined' to stop Chalmraik."

"Isn't Chalmraik dead?" one of the infants asked.

"Wizards don't die, ever'body knows *that*," the other said. "I heard he was on some island somewheres."

"So did these two shitbrains," Horran said. "And they *both*—not one, but both—fell for the Runes of Tyrac scam."

"Looks like an epidemic of heroism," Danthres muttered.

"Yeah, I heard about Brightblade when I brought the two morons in," said Horran. "You and Lieutenant ban Wyvald caught that one?"

Danthres nodded. "The good news is we get unlimited overtime, and we plan to take every advantage."

Horran laughed. "No wonder you were so late comin' in."

One infant whispered to the other one, "Maybe she can make enough to buy a new face."

No doubt the guard made the comment secure in the knowledge that no one could possibly have heard him aside from his friend. Danthres debated whether or not it was worth pursuing—she had been in a bad mood all day because of this damned murder, but the overtime revelation had improved it a bit.

Oh, why not? "Did you say something, child?"

The infant's face went whiter than a vampire's. "Uh, n-no, Lieutenant, not a—not a thing. Really. Honest."

"Good. Because if you *had* said what I thought I heard you clearly say, it would be *you* requiring a new face, not me."

Urgoss then came over with the four flagons,

which were now filled with the house ale. "On the tab?" he said.

"Of course." Aside from Grovis—who usually went straight back home to Mommy and Daddy's mansion in Unicorn when the shift ended, no doubt to regale the family with exaggerated tales of his exploits over brandy and cigars—all the lieutenants on their shift came to the Chain virtually every night, so Urgoss was more than happy to let them build up a tab, to be paid on the first day of the new month, which was payday.

She curled her fingers through two flagon handles each and gingerly lifted them off the wooden bar. Inclining her head at Horran, and ignoring the other two, she walked slowly toward the back.

" 'Ey, look, Tresyllione's fin'ly here!"

Lord and Lady, no. She kept walking toward her table even as she knew she would be stopped by the body attached to the drunken, slurred voice.

Sure enough, the oversized head, overweight body, misshapen face, and patchy curled hair of Nulti interposed itself between Danthres and her destination. She was amazed to see that he had actually gained more weight since she saw him last, his protuberant belly looking like it was about to burst through his leather armor. As it was, the goblin emblem on the chest looked a bit stretched.

"Sergeant Markon finally let you back on his shift, Nulti?"

" 'Ey, I *earned* m'way back t'days, Tresyllione.

Don't need to go suckin' off the boss t'get a promotion."

"The way you drool, Nulti, sucking off the boss would get you a demotion."

To Danthres's amusement, Nulti actually ran his bread-loaf-sized forearm across his mouth at that. " 'Ey, lissen, got a bet goin' with m'buddies over 'ere." He indicated a table, where half a dozen foot soldiers from Goblin were sitting, drinking, laughing, probably at her expense, and watching their conversation. She didn't know any of them—they had probably signed up after her promotion to lieutenant. Besides, they looked young and stupid, and hadn't yet acquired the hard edge that patrolling Goblin gave you after a few years.

"Nulti, I don't have—" she started, attempting to push past the oaf, but his portly frame blocked the only path to her table.

"See, ev'yone knows fr'm lookin' atcher shit-ugly face 'atcher half-elf. What we got to bettin' 'bout is what th'other half is. Me, I say it's troll. Other guys, 'ey say it's dwarf. So we wantcha t'settle'a bet."

Then Nulti let out a long, loud guffaw, which was echoed by his fellows.

The rest of the tavern started to grow quiet.

Danthres sighed. Nulti had been riding her since she signed up. Few women joined the Guard, and those that did generally had some kind of formal combat training and experience. Danthres had none of the former, and the latter consisted primarily of brawls with people who took offense at Danthres's face, personality, or both. To make matters worse, the boss was Captain Brisban, a veteran of the elven wars who hated elves and thought women had *no* place in the Guard, prior experience notwithstanding. So instead of a simple beat to walk in Unicorn, she was instead posted to the sewer that was Goblin Precinct, no doubt in the hopes of her washing out quickly. Danthres took pride in the fact that she dashed those hopes rather handily.

Nulti wasn't the only one to give her a constant stream of shit, but he was the loudest and second most obnoxious after Brisban himself. But, over a decade later, Brisban was dead, Danthres was promoted to the castle, and Nulti was still stuck in Goblin. He was insufficiently competent to be promoted, insufficiently incompetent to be fired, and his corruption was so run-of-the-mill and low-stakes that he wasn't worth the effort to investigate.

I really don't want to start a fight tonight, she thought.

"Well, c'mon, Tresyllione, which is it? Got me three coppers ridin' on ya bein' troll—that's 'cause'a your disposition—but Afrak over 'ere, 'e says 'at it's dwarf on account'a hearin' that you suck in bed. Dunno who'e coulda heard *'at* from, seein' as how no one sane'd sleep with y'anyhow, and—"

Whatever Nulti was going to say next was lost as Danthres upended all four flagons of ale onto his huge, round head. His random patches of curly hair straightened, and ale dripped off his flat face, his big ears, and his small nose into his big mouth, which was hanging open.

Now the Chain filled with laughter, loudest of all coming from Nulti's own fellows.

Nulti continued to stand in place, his mouth hanging open, though he did blink twice.

Danthres turned around and noticed that Urgoss wasn't laughing. Then again, he never did, but he was probably already calculating the cost of the damage that the impending fight would inflict, which he'd bill to Osric, and which Osric would bill to her and Nulti. *I'll probably wind up paying him most of my overtime money.*

"Half-breed *bitch!*"

Not even needing to turn back around to see what Nulti was doing, Danthres knew that the oaf was now charging at her, ready to throw a punch. So she ducked down into a crouch. Nulti stumbled, his intended target having all but disappeared, his girth causing him to fall forward—onto her. Danthres held up her hands, catching him at the chest, his great weight pressing down on her. She was able to support his weight, however, and then straightened to an upright position, throwing Nulti backward. His weight and drunken clumsiness combined to make that upright pose a temporary one, and he fell all the way over, back-first into one of the empty chairs, his head colliding with the table, knocking over several drinks. He then sat there, sprawled and unmoving, a combination of drool and ale dripping out of his still-hanging-open mouth.

One of the people sitting at that table, whose wine was now on the floor, asked, "Is he dead?"

"We can only hope," Danthres said.

Torin, who, she now noticed, was standing nearby, along with Dru and Hawk, added, "But he only hit his head, so it wasn't like any vital organs were harmed." Then he grinned. "I'm hurt. You gave him my drink."

"You'll get over it." She turned to the bar. "Four more, please, Urgoss, and refill these people's drinks on me."

"Thanks," said the wine-drinker, a young guard from Unicorn. "For what it's worth, I like the way you look. It's—exotic." He even waggled his eyebrows for effect.

"Oh, for Wiate's sake, Manfred," one of his comrades, also from Unicorn, said, "not again. Didn't you get in enough trouble after what happened at the stable?"

Oh Lord and Lady, not another thrill-seeker. One of the reasons why Danthres had chosen Torin as an occasional lover was because he was fond of *her*. The only people who had expressed any interest in her physically were those who were attracted by her status as a half-breed. Half-elves who were permitted to live past the age of one day were rare this far north—indeed, Danthres had seen plenty of mass graves of half-breed infants in the nearby elven lands before she came to Cliff's End—and she had dealt with more than her share of those who wanted, as one propositioner had put it, "the half-elf experience."

That particular man soon learned that "the half-elf experience" consisted primarily of broken bones in his sword arm and a smashed nose.

Suddenly, the air in the Chain was weighing her down. *I need to get out of here.* She turned to Torin. "I'm leaving. I'll see you tomorrow morning."

"Of course," Torin said with a nod. Danthres was grateful that he didn't raise a fuss that she was rescinding her earlier invite, but after all this, the last thing she wanted to do was take Torin home. Even though she knew Torin would never treat it as such, his sleeping with her tonight would feel like nothing more than a sympathy fuck, and she simply couldn't stand that on top of everything else.

" 'Scuse me, but, uh—"

Danthres looked over at the entrance to see a guard from Dragon standing in the doorway. "Yes?"

He pointed at the dripping, prone form of Nulti. "That ain't Lieutenant ban Wyvald, is it?"

"Hardly," Torin said. "I am."

"Good. So you're Lieutenant Tresyllione. You both gotta come with me."

"We're off until sunup," Danthres said. "Can't this wait?"

" 'Fraid not, ma'am. Got a directive when we came on from Cap'n Osric sayin' that to find you two if something happened related to the Brightblade murder, an' Sergeant Kel takes them directives serious, ma'am."

Running the words *unlimited overtime* through her head like a mantra, Danthres asked, "What happened?"

"Another body at the Dog and Duck, ma'am."

The dead body this time was Olthar lothSirhans, the elf. Torin knew his story by heart—most everyone who lived under King Marcus and Queen Marta's rule did. The nephew of the Elf Queen, Olthar was one of the heroes of the elven wars for betraying his aunt, which led to the humans' victory. Without that sacrifice, it was quite likely that they'd all be speaking the elven tongue right now.

During his interview of Olthar following Brightblade's murder, Torin was made quickly aware that the elf knew the importance of his role in that war, and that it made him above such petty concerns as answering questions about the death of one of his comrades. The uncharitable side of Torin thought that Olthar's death was on his own head for being uncooperative.

The crime scene was more or less the equivalent of the last one: Olthar's lodgings, in Room 13. This room was the mirror image of Brightblade's—the desk on the north side instead of the south, the bed against the west wall rather than the east, and so on.

The other primary difference was the location of

the body. Where Brightblade had fallen in the middle of the floor, the elf was seated, slumped over onto the desk, a quill in his left hand. His head—which, like Brightblade's, was at an off angle from the rest of his body—rested on a piece of parchment. Torin peered in to see impeccable handwriting, in the flourish-heavy script of the eastern elves.

He looked over at his partner. "I don't suppose you know Ra-Telvish?"

"Speak, yes—read, no. Literacy wasn't exactly a prime concern when I was a child, and by the time I was old enough to teach myself, I stuck with Common." She joined Torin at the table. "No finger marks on *his* neck, either. And the quill is near the end of a character." She frowned. "I do know this much—that's the middle of a word. *Vrasheth,* I think, or maybe *vranth*. Something like that—in any case, he was caught off-guard in midsentence."

"Just like Brightblade." Torin sighed. "It looks like it isn't just a single murder—someone's targeting this entire group." He turned to the guard standing in the doorway. "Who found the body?"

"Dwarf," the guard said.

He turned to Danthres. "I think we both should talk to him."

Danthres nodded. "Definitely." She looked over at the guard. "Where is he?"

"Who?"

Closing her eyes and sighing, Danthres said, "The dwarf."

"Oh. Next door. His room."

"Someone *is* watching him, I hope?" Torin asked.

The guard nodded.

"Good. Any word on when the M.E. will arrive?"

The guard shrugged.

Danthres stared at Torin. "He didn't even send a mage-bird?"

"Well, it's the middle of the night. We'll be lucky if he even shows up." Then he grinned. "Three coppers says he isn't here until sunup."

Snorting, Danthres said, "No bet. I'll be stunned if he's here before midday tomorrow. Come on, let's talk to the dwarf."

Ubàrlig was staying in Room 14, which had the same design as Brightblade's. The dwarf, however, had added some personal touches, even though it was only supposed to be a short stay. His Fjorm axe was now hanging from one wall, and several poorly sculpted figurines of dwarves in assorted bizarre positions were festooned about the desk and on the nightstand beside the basin.

The dwarf himself sat on the floor next to the bed, mending a hole in his tunic. Tall by the standards of his race, Ubàrlig still only came up to Torin's chest. His hairline had receded to the back of his head, but he still grew his light brown hair well past shoulder length in the back, with a beard of equivalent length in the same hue. His nose was small, but with a bulbous tip, and his blue eyes of surprisingly good humor for a war veteran of his years.

"Good evening, General," Torin said formally as the guard let him into the room. "I'm sorry we have to speak again so soon under such horrible circumstances."

"That's okay, Lieutenant." Ubàrlig rose from the floor. "I was just doing something with my hands." He set the tunic down on the bed.

Torin looked at the figures. "I would think you'd be sculpting to do that."

The dwarf laughed. "Ain't got the right material for *that*. I didn't bring clay with me, and there ain't no kilns out on the Garamin, far as I know, so I can't fire the stuff, neither. The plan's to take a nice sea cruise, so I didn't think it'd be a hot idea to bring 'em along. Nah, I just brought this stuff for laughs—mine, and the rest of the gang, since they like to make fun of my sculptin'," Ubàrlig added with a self-deprecating grin.

"I'm sure they only have your best interests at heart." Torin then blinked, as if he had momentarily forgotten Danthres. "Oh! This is my partner, Lieutenant Tresyllione."

Ubàrlig looked at her for a moment, seeming to study her face. "You're from Sorlin, right?"

Danthres smiled most unpleasantly. "I'm from Guard Headquarters, Mr. Ubàrlig, and we're investigating two murders."

The dwarf moved to sit on the chair next to the desk. "Murders? Since when? I thought Gan died by accident."

"A final determination hasn't been made, but given the circumstances," Torin said, "I do not believe we are jumping to an irrational conclusion. We're told you found Mr. lothSirhans's body."

"Yes, I did. He was supposed to come to dinner with me and Genero, and he was late. Typical, really—Ears got *no* sense of time—" he said, using a common dwarven slang term to refer to elves, "—and Olthar was lousy even by their standards. He wasn't on time for a damn thing in the hundred and fifty years he was alive. But two hours late for dinner is pretty bad even for him. So I came up to see what the hell was keeping him. The door was open, so I came in. You know what I found."

Torin nodded. "Was it unusual for the door to be open?"

The dwarf shook his head. "As your partner probably knows," he said with a glance at Danthres, "Ears got *no* concept of locks."

We're all aware, Torin thought with amusement. Elves new to human lands were often easy marks for thieves. During the massive immigration of elven refugees that followed the wars, the Guard had to set up a special task force just to deal with elves who were robbery victims. However, Torin would have thought someone who had lived among humans as long as lothSirhans had would have known better. *Then again, perhaps the hero of the elven wars thought himself above such petty concerns.*

Ubàrlig picked up one of the figurines and stared

at it for a moment. "Olthar's a great man, Lieutenants. Was, anyhow. Look, there's not a single Ear, living or dead, about whom I'd even consider saying something nice, much less call great. For Olthar, though, I'll say and for damn sure mean it. I can count on one hand how many people I'd gladly give my life for. Two of 'em have died in this inn."

"In that case, General," Torin said, "you should want to help us find out who killed them. You must have some common enemies."

"Not still alive. Unless there's some long-lost relative or devotee of the Elf Queen." The dwarf rubbed his bearded chin. "That's actually a pretty good possibility. The Elf Queen had tons of followers—stands to reason that one or two of them may still be alive and are holding a grudge. Both Gan and Olthar were *big* thorns in her side."

Torin had to admit that that was a possibility. There were no other elves staying at the Dog and Duck, but that didn't mean anything in and of itself. It was certainly worth pursuing. "What about the others?"

"What about 'em?"

"Well, might they also be targets of the Elf Queen's wrath?"

The dwarf smiled. "None of us have any love lost for her, if that's what you mean. Well, except for Mari and Nari. They didn't have anything to do with the elven wars at all."

"Then what are they doing with your group?" Danthres asked.

Ubàrlig laughed. "I been wonderin' that myself, Lieutenant. But Brother Genero has a history with them, and they're pretty useful, though pretty damn irritating when you get right down to it. But nah, the Elf Queen probably didn't have a clue who they are. But they haven't been targeted, either. The rest of us, though, she hated all our guts. One of those nut-cases that followed her could've decided to get revenge on her behalf."

Just as Torin was about to ask his next question, a voice sounded from behind him. "General Ubàrlig, here you are!"

The speaker had used a full sentence, so it couldn't have been the guard. And indeed, it wasn't; the man who spoke was half a head shorter than the guard—who had apparently let him in. He wore a hat that was the height of fashion at court in the castle, and that no one would be caught dead wearing anywhere but there or Unicorn. His silk tunic and breeches were covered by a billowing cloak that, Torin suspected, was mostly to keep out the filth, both inanimate and living.

After a moment, Torin placed the face of the man as belonging to Sir Rommett, the chamberlain at Lord Albin and Lady Meerka's court, and a man with sufficient clout that an errand to such a place as the Dog and Duck *had* to be beneath his station. He had people for that sort of thing.

Which means that this case is about to get far more complicated.

"It's my room," Ubàrlig said with a snort. "Where the hell else *would* I be?"

"I've come to convey you and your friends—"

If Danthres recognized Rommett, she didn't show it—or, more likely, didn't care—as she interrupted him. "Get this man out of here!" she snapped at the guard.

"I beg your pardon! Don't you know who I am?"

"You're not in uniform, so you're not a member of the Guard. Are you a witness to either of the murders that took place in this inn?"

Rommett drew himself up to his full height—which wasn't much more than that of Ubàrlig. "Of course not! I've never set foot in this—this *establishment* before tonight, and I hope never to have to—"

"In that case, you're a civilian trespassing on a crime scene." With a pointed look at the guard—who seemed completely uninterested in the proceedings—she added, "You should never have been let in here in the first place."

"Danthres—" Torin started.

"My dear lady—"

"I'm not a lady," Danthres said, and Torin had to bite his tongue to keep from making a comment on that, "I'm a lieutenant in the Cliff's End Castle Guard, and you're trespassing on my crime scene."

"Not for much longer you aren't." Rommett reached into the folds of his cloak and pulled out his seal of office. "I am Sir Rommett, the chamberlain of Cliff's End. Your pet thugs let me into this pit of an inn because I carry this seal. I am here on official business of the city-state, which is to convey the general here, as well as Brother Genero and the rest of their party, to the castle, where they will remain as guests of the Lord and Lady until this matter is concluded."

"Good Sir Rommett," Torin said quickly before Danthres got them into more trouble, "that stay will be indefinite unless we are allowed to do our work. We need to question General Ubàrlig as well as—"

"Nonsense. He's a victim here, not—"

Danthres snarled. "He found the body."

Speaking as if to a child, Rommett said, "Then he *obviously* isn't the perpetrator."

Ubàrlig chose that moment to speak up. "I'm perfectly happy to help the lieutenants out, Sir Rommett."

His tone turning obsequious, Rommett said, "Oh, of course you are, General, of course you are, but that can wait, I'm sure. We have a carriage downstairs, along with a full escort of guards to ensure your safe passage. The guards were handpicked by Captain Osric himself." He looked up at Danthres, and the obsequiousness gave way to a harder tone. "Your supervisor, if memory serves. I will be speaking with him soon, of that you can rest assured, *Lieutenant*. I suggest you go home and figure out what line of work is available to a woman of your severely limited charm and good looks, because I can assure you that the Guard will *not* be an option for you much longer."

Torin grabbed Danthres by the arm and shook his head quickly, before she could react. *Don't make this any worse than it already is,* he thought as fervently as he could. As it was, if Osric had been forced to assemble an escort in the middle of the night, he was going to be sharpening his dagger down to the size of a toothpick come sunup.

Within moments, Ubàrlig had collected a few changes of clothes, his figurines, and his axe, and Rommett brought him downstairs. Before leaving, the dwarf assured Torin that he would continue to cooperate in any way necessary.

As soon as the door shut behind them, Danthres pounded a fist on the desk. "I'm still waiting for him to *start* cooperating! And now *this!*"

"It's not surprising," Torin said. "When it was just Brightblade, and it looked like it at least *might* be an accident, that was one thing. But there's no way lothSirhans accidentally snapped his own neck while composing a letter. And he *is* Olthar lothSirhans."

Danthres waved him off. "Yes, yes, I know, the great hero who went against the wishes of his aunt the Elf Queen, and so on. I've heard the story *endlessly.*"

"Yes, and without that betrayal, we would have lost that war. Lord Albin and Lady Meerka owe their very position to that betrayal."

"So their solution is to come in and make it *harder* to find the murderer?"

Torin couldn't help but grin. "Of course. It's what the upper classes do best."

Danthres barked out a laugh. "How do you do that?"

"What?"

"Make me laugh when it's the last thing I want to do?"

"Ten years of practice."

Shaking her head, Danthres turned to the guard. "You. Find someone intimidating and send him to the castle to fetch the M.E. I don't care if he has to bodily drag him over here by his ankles, I want that peel-back *now*. If we can't talk to witnesses, we're damn well going to have *something* by sunup."

"Indeed." Torin followed the guard out the door. "I'm going to go downstairs and see if there are any actual witnesses."

Danthres actually smiled at that. "Three coppers says you don't find any."

That caused Torin to laugh as he headed for the hallway. "Since you still owe me from earlier, I'll take it."

He was pretty sure he had seen the man with the leather armor and the beard before. Yes, the last time he cast the spells before tonight. Or shortly afterward. Or something.

But he had spoken to the man with the beard

then, definitely. The bearded man looked a bit like the old man who had saved him. Except, of course, the old man had white hair and didn't wear leather armor.

But otherwise, they looked a lot alike.

"That's a very nice design," he said to the bearded man. "On your chest, I mean. I've never seen anything like it before."

"It's a gryphon," the bearded man said. "It means that I work out of Guard headquarters in the castle."

"Castle?"

"Lord Albin and Lady Meerka's castle," the bearded man said slowly.

"Oh, right, of course, the castle. You'll have to excuse me. I'm afraid that my memory isn't what it used to be."

The bearded man smiled. "Whose is, truly?"

He laughed at that. "Good point, very good point, yes, indeed. Er, what was your question?"

"Did you see anything odd or suspicious tonight involving the elf who was staying here?"

Now he had to choose his words carefully. "Not specifically. Just that he went up to his room and closed the door. The only odd thing was that dwarf going up the stairs and knocking on his door a couple hours later. Thought that was odd, I tell you."

"Why is that?"

Be careful, don't let him know what you know, because then he'll know it and all will be lost! "He's a dwarf. Dwarves and elves don't usually mix, you know?"

"True. Aside from when you saw him go upstairs, had you seen the elf at all during the evening?"

"No," he lied.

The bearded man asked a few more questions. He tried to answer them as best he could without giving anything away.

He couldn't afford to give anything away. Not until it was all finished. Then it would be done. Yes, all done. Then all the debts would have been paid and he could get on with what he wanted to get on with.

"Good sir?"

"Hm?" He looked up to see the bearded man looking at him expectantly. "What is it?"

"You haven't answered my question."

"I'm sorry, what was it?"

"How long did the dwarf spend in the room?"

"Oh, I'm honestly not sure. Some kind of ruckus was raised, but I honestly don't know how long it was."

"You don't recall when the last time-chime was?"

"I'm afraid I don't pay them much heed, really. I don't even notice them, to be honest." *Besides, time has become so fluid . . .*

"Understandable." The bearded man leaned forward and spoke in an almost confidential tone. "I have to confess, I'm barely aware of them myself. So you spent the entire evening in the dining area?"

"Yes. The stew wasn't bad at all." Then he smiled.

"Actually, the stew was terrible, but the ale was good, so that made the stew better, too."

They both laughed at that. The bearded man—who looked so much like the old man it was almost frightening—then thanked him, told him to contact a guard if he remembered anything else, and departed.

He went back to his room after that. His work wasn't nearly complete yet.

Four

Manfred sighed as he walked his post on the streets of Unicorn Precinct, wishing that the Guard would approve the concept of a summer-weight uniform.

Humidity was a near constant in Cliff's End, but this morning, the moisture content was almost unbearable—especially to someone covered shoulders-to-boots in leather armor. He just knew he was going to have all manner of entertaining rashes and such when he changed out of his armor—which he intended to do the second he got off shift. As it was, he was already starting to itch in spots he would not be able to scratch for another eleven hours at least.

If I'm lucky, today will be another quiet day. And if I'm even luckier, Lieutenant Tresyllione will be at the Chain again tonight.

With a smile, he thought back on how she took

care of that jackass from Goblin. She was a joy to watch, turning her back on Nulti and *still* taking him out. Of course, Manfred and the other three had to move to a different table—Nulti tended to carry an odor around with him even when he wasn't completely drunk and dripping wet with ale—but it was worth it to watch that amazing woman in action. True, she was not the most traditionally attractive person in Flingaria, but most of those who were used glamours in any case. To find someone as odd-featured as that yet who was sufficiently comfortable in her own skin to not make any of the easily available adjustments—*that* turned Manfred on.

Now, if only I can get her *to see that, and how I feel about her. . . .*

To Manfred's irritation, neither of his desires were likely to come to fruition today. Sergeant Arron had said at roll call that all the day-shift detectives had big cases, so unless a body fell, they would have to deal with any hard cases themselves. And since Lieutenant Tresyllione and her partner had caught both the Brightblade murder and last night's murder of Olthar lothSirhans, he doubted she'd be having much time to socialize at the Chain.

Manfred actually had less of a problem with the lack of availability of the detectives than some others did. He never liked the fact that they always had to call in one of the lieutenants, as if none of the foot soldiers had a brain in their heads. True, several of them didn't—Nulti was a classic case—but Manfred liked to think he was capable of solving a robbery or an assault case. *Maybe today I'll get my chance.*

He turned a corner onto Shade Way, a turn he made primarily for the reason the street was so named. The road was lined by several huge oak trees. It didn't help much with the humidity, of course, but at least the morning sun wasn't bearing down on him on this cloudless day. The houses on Shade Way were more of the mansion variety, the homes of the idle rich, of which Cliff's End had its share. Certainly, Manfred was unlikely to find any criminal activity here, but even rich people had domestic disputes, or noise complaints, or other such need for the Guard's services. Besides, in the shade, his arms stopped itching.

"Excuse me?"

Manfred turned around quickly, his arm going to his sword hilt instinctively. However, the speaker was a young man, probably in his late teens or early twenties, dressed in casual clothes that were inexpensive, but not cheap. The boy looked down at the ground as he spoke. *Probably a servant in one of the mansions*, Manfred thought, proud of his ability to deduce.

"Are—are you a guard?" the boy asked, still studying the cobblestones intently.

No, I stole this armor. Manfred managed to restrain himself from saying that out loud, however. "Yes. What can I do for you?"

"My—my mistress asked me to fetch a guard,

and—and you're a guard, so—so I guess I need for you to come with me, sir."

"Lead on, then," he said.

The boy brought Manfred back to the corner where he'd turned onto Shade Way, to a massive house that had obviously been built some time in the last twenty years or so, after the humans and dwarves allied, and dwarven architects peddled their wares outside their own territory. Manfred's late father had been an architect, and from him the guard knew that you could tell a dwarf-designed house by the lack of a second floor. Everything was ground-level or below. Manfred's father had taught his son this, usually while cursing those "sawed-off runts" for "taking work away from honest humans." However, what dwarven architecture lacked in height, it made up for in structural integrity, as many Cliff's End natives learned after the last hurricane blew through the city-state.

From what Manfred could see as the boy led him down the walkway around to the back of the house, the structure had at least fifteen rooms, all on the ground floor, and if he knew his dwarves, then there were probably almost as many rooms one or two levels down. As he walked around to the back, he noticed that the brick was not the usual Aemrian that the dwarves favored, but the lesser Cambrian variety—not as sturdy, but easier to find. Manfred wondered if the architect had duped the owner, or if the owner had gone cheap.

All thoughts of the house fled Manfred's mind as soon as he came in sight of the lush backyard—which was marred by a large hole, about three dwarf-lengths in diameter. Peculiarly for a hole, it was in the middle of the air about three hand-lengths above the impeccably cut grass. Amber in color, the hole was a perfect circle above the ground. The amber seemed to swirl, looking to Manfred like butter being churned. *Must be magic. Maybe a portal of some kind?* Manfred didn't know much about magic beyond its existence—anytime he came across it, the case got kicked up to the lieutenants, and it almost always got kicked up from there to the Brotherhood of Wizards.

Still, he needed to do some kind of investigating. The first thing he did was go around to the other side of the hole—which was easy, as the hole wasn't much thicker than a piece of parchment. To his disappointment, it looked exactly the same on the other side. It was as if someone had taken a massive amber coin and suspended it in midair over the lawn.

"Oh, thank Temisa."

Manfred turned to see a woman wearing a cotton dress, followed by two young women wearing simple outfits similar to what the boy was wearing. *The lady of the house,* he deduced, again proud of his observational capacity. *Just you wait, Lieutenant Tresyllione, we'll be serving side by side before you know it.*

"I hope you're here to help me," the woman added.

"Yes, ma'am. Name's Manfred, ma'am. And you are?"

She held out her hand to be kissed. Manfred knew that upper-class women liked that sort of thing, though he had always found it silly. Still, it was expected, and the sergeant had drilled into them that they were to always do what was expected, so he kissed the hand as she said, "I am Elmira Fansarri, and I am a close personal friend of Lady Meerka's, so I expected this to be dealt with *quickly*, or she shall hear of it."

Meaning you met Lady Meerka once at a party. Still, Manfred recognized the Fansarri name, and they weren't without clout. "I take it, Madame Fansarri, that this, ah, this—hole isn't supposed to be there?"

"I should say *not*," Elmira said. She was moderately attractive, Manfred supposed, though wearing far more makeup than was necessary—and on this humid day, some of it was caked or running. Manfred wondered why she didn't just use a glamour like most people. Instead, she looked like one of those wretched actors who performed in the park during the spring. Manfred had had to endure several performances of *The Ballad of King Ytrehod* a few months back while making sure that the crowds didn't riot during or after the performances—which, given the quality of the performance, was a very real risk.

The sad thing is, she probably has dozens of suitors who vie for her time while her husband's away.

Putting that in the back of his mind, he asked the question he knew Lieutenant Tresyllione would ask if she were here. "What happened?"

"How in Temisa's name should *I* know?" Elmira said angrily. "Why do you think I told Willard to find *you?*"

Sighing, Manfred tried a more direct approach. "When did you first notice the hole in your yard?"

"About ten minutes ago when I happened to look out the window, and there it was! Now are you going to stop wasting time asking me questions and *do* something about it, or do I have to find someone who *will?* I'm good friends with Lady Meerka, you know, and I can assure you that she'll hear about this shoddy treatment!"

"Ma'am," Manfred said with all the patience he could muster, "I can't do anything about the situation until I know what happened. I have to ask questions first—that's the proper procedure for me to do my job. I'm sure that you and Lady Meerka would prefer that I did my job right, right?" *Ouch. That sounded bad.* "This is probably magical—in origin, I mean."

"Any idiot can see *that.*"

"Do you know any wizards, ma'am?"

"Oh Temisa, no! I hate wizards. Last one we had over for a dinner party nearly ruined the whole thing. No, I won't hear of having one of those arrogant, overbearing creatures in my house!"

Aha! A clue. And that also explains why she wears makeup instead of using a glamour. "When was this dinner party, ma'am?"

Elmira looked at Manfred as if he had grown a second head. "I beg your pardon?"

"Well, ma'am, if you had a bad experience with a wizard and let him know about that—or even if you didn't, but if he found out that you carried this grudge against his kind because of his behavior—then that might be a motive for why he might decide to put a portal of some sort into your backyard. See, ma'am, this is why it's necessary to ask questions, so we can get at the truth of why—"

In a tight voice, Elmira said, "It was ten years ago. The wizard in question died five years ago."

Manfred felt deflated. *Damn. It was a good theory, too.*

The woman reached out a hand, and one of the girls standing behind her handed her a handkerchief. She dabbed it irritably over her forehead, which was beaded with sweat and caked makeup. "Now if you do not stop wasting my time—"

"Who else is present in the house?" Manfred asked before she could cite her friendship with Lady Meerka again.

"We're all standing right here!" Elmira practically screamed the words. "Just me and these three servants—and the cook, but she's out at market. All the rest of the servants are with my husband—he took them on his business trip to Iaron, and he won't be back until next month." Then her face softened. "Oh, well, there's also my dear son, but he's in his room. He's been there all day, of course." She shook her head. "He's a teenager, he—"

Whatever else Elmira was going to say about her son was lost by a screeching sound coming from the portal. Manfred turned around to see that the swirls of amber were now rotating faster—and changing color to a more red hue. "Something's happening," he said, his hand moving to his sword hilt.

"Another brilliant observation," Elmira said snidely. "I *do* wonder what my taxes are paying for. I will have to bring it up with Lady Meerka when next I speak to her. We're *very* good friends, you know."

So I've heard. Manfred bit back the retort. Instead, he peered more closely at the hole. There seemed to be movement, and he was hearing some kind of noise. It almost seemed to be laughter.

A moment later, a diminutive creature with orange fur covering all of its body save its yellow face came leaping out of the portal, cackling madly.

"Hobgoblin!" Manfred cried, unsheathing his sword and interposing himself between the creature and the civilians. "Get behind me!"

"We're already behind you, you idiot! Kill that thing!"

The servants, for their part, just screamed.

Manfred had heard all about hobgoblins—they were on the chart on the bulletin board—but had never seen one. They generally didn't come this far north, though Manfred had a friend who was in Tomvale when the town was overrun six years ago. If he remembered correctly, they preferred to grab whatever weapon came to hand and beat their prey over the head until they stopped moving.

The one advantage Manfred had was that the impeccable lawn had no such weapons—no stray branches or rocks, not even dirt clods. While the hobgoblin wasted time looking for something, Manfred charged and swung his sword at it.

Unfortunately, hobgoblins were also quite fast. This one dashed to the left at the last second, leaving Manfred to stumble forward in much the same way Nulti had the previous night. Eyes widening, he realized he was about to go into the portal, and he managed to stop himself, but at the cost of his balance, and he fell down.

Struggling to his feet, he wondered what Elmira would complain about more, his ineptitude or the fact that he had matted down some of her perfectly manicured lawn.

Looking up, he saw that such was the least of Elmira Fansarri's problems: the hobgoblin was heading straight for her. She was now also screaming, and apparently so scared that she was rooted to the spot. Her servants, at least, had the wherewithal to run away—Manfred could see their retreating forms moving toward the house. *They'll probably head for one of the basements.*

Manfred ran toward the hobgoblin even as it

knocked Elmira to the ground. Her screams mingled with the hobgoblin's cackling to form a shrill cacophony even as the hobgoblin started to beat the wealthy woman about the head and shoulders. Not having found a useful weapon for the task, the creature was using its hands.

As he ran toward the tableau, Manfred wondered if he should say something as he attacked. Someone like Gan Brightblade would probably cry out, "Have at you!"

On the other hand, Lieutenant Tresyllione would probably just stab the thing in the back.

As the hobgoblin's long arms collided with the side of Elmira's head, Manfred ran it through. Green ichor spurted all over the lawn, Manfred's uniform, and Elmira herself, with more doing so when he pulled the weapon out. The hobgoblin collapsed on top of the woman, dead.

"TemisaTemisaTemisagetthisthingoffmeNOW!"

Smiling, Manfred rolled the creature off the woman, then offered her a hand up.

"Don't you dare touch me! Do you see what that thing *did* to me! I'm going to report you to Lady Meerka! She's my friend, you know, and she will boil you in oil for allowing this to happen to me! Ardra! Ardra! Where *is* that damned girl? *Ardra!*"

Manfred saw one of the girls' heads peeking out from one of the mansion's back doors. He assumed this was Ardra. "It's all right," he called out. "The hobgoblin's dead. It's safe."

"There is nothing *safe* in this place until *you* are gone!"

Ignoring her, and leaving her on the ground, since she seemed unwilling to get up on her own or accept his help, Manfred turned—to see that the portal was gone. *I guess it did what it was supposed to do.* He also noted that a strip of grass right under where the portal had been was completely flattened.

All right, Manfred, think this through the way Lieutenant Tresyllione would. A magic portal that brings hobgoblins into backyards doesn't happen naturally. Someone had to cast a spell. It obviously wasn't the lady of the house. One of the servants?

He turned to Ardra, who was helping the ichor-stained Elmira to her feet. "Excuse me, Ardra? Can you or any of the other two servants here read?"

Before Ardra could answer, Elmira said, "What a ridiculous question! My handservants have no need to *read.*"

That leaves them out, he thought. *Magic requires literacy. Of course, one of them could secretly be reading on the side. I'll need to talk to them out of the way of Madame Fansarri. So if it isn't any of them . . .*

Then he remembered that there was someone else in the house.

He caught up to Elmira and Ardra, who were now walking toward the house. "I need to talk to your son."

"Whatever *for?* My dear Oswalt is an angel, but

he's also very sensitive. I don't want a thug like you talking to him."

"Perhaps, but he might have seen something. It's procedure, ma'am. As I said before—"

Waving her arms about, Elmira said, "Of course, your *precious* procedure. If you *must* talk to my son, go ahead, but be *gentle* with him—not like you were with that hobgoblin. Honestly, such brutality."

Again, Manfred had to bite back his instinctive answer. *I'm sorry you don't like the way I killed the creature that was about to beat you to a bloody pulp, ma'am.*

She cried out, "Willard!"

The boy who had brought Manfred to the house ran up to her, in his usual position of staring at the ground.

"Go fetch Oswalt, boy."

"Yes'm."

Before he could run off, Manfred said, "And Willard? When you've done that, I need you to go to Unicorn Precinct headquarters and speak to Sergeant Arron—tell him I sent for you and that we have a dead hobgoblin that needs to be disposed of. He'll take care of things."

"Yessir." Then the boy ran off to the house to fetch the boy.

As Manfred, Elmira, and Ardra approached the mansion at a more leisurely pace, the lady of the house bellowed, "Stop right there! Talk to my son if you must, but I won't have you tracking your filth into my home! You may speak to him *out here.*"

The part of Manfred that was the son of an architect longed to see the inside of the dwarf-designed mansion, but the part that was a guard decided it was just as well, since he'd be separated from Elmira if he remained outdoors.

He also noted that she had no trouble tracking her *own* filth—which was of considerably greater quantity than his—into the house. But then, it was *her* house, and it had a bath that she no doubt intended to make use of. Manfred felt a temporary pang of jealousy.

Within a few minutes, a tall, gangly teenaged boy exited into the yard to join Manfred. He walked awkwardly, as if he wasn't comfortable in his own skin, and he didn't quite know what to do with his arms. *Probably just hit his growth spurt,* Manfred thought, again proud of his observational prowess. "You must be Oswalt."

"Yeah."

"My name's Manfred. I'm with the Guard, and I need to ask you some questions."

"'Kay."

"Did you see what happened out here?"

He shrugged.

"Do you know who cast the spell that caused that portal to open?"

Another shrug.

"Any wizards sneaking around?"

"Wizards don't sneak."

Manfred frowned. "You know about wizards?"

"Some."

"How?"

Yet another shrug. "Readin'."

"You read a lot?"

"Some. An' I hear stuff."

"What kind of stuff do you hear?"

"Just stuff. 'Bout wizards."

"Like what?"

A fifth shrug. "They're nasty. Like Chalmraik."

Manfred chuckled. "Chalmraik's dead."

"Maybe. Never know with wizards."

This was getting Manfred nowhere. "That hobgoblin beat up your mother pretty good."

A sixth shrug.

Not filled with love for Mother. Hardly surprising, given the mother in question.

Then, suddenly, it all fell together for Manfred.

"You cast the spell, didn't you?"

Up until Manfred asked that question, Oswalt had been competing with Willard for first prize in the stare-at-the-ground competition. At that query, however, his head shot up. "I—I can't cast no spells. I—I ain't no wizard! Honest! I can't do nothin' like that!"

Manfred almost jumped with glee. *Did it! Hah! Case solved!*

True, he still had to go through the motions. He had to search the boy's room to find the scrolls—*if he's anything like I was as a teenager, he's got them under his bed*—and then arrest him, and then listen to Elmira wail on about how her little boy couldn't *possibly* be mixed up in this, there must be some mistake, I'm going to talk to my *good friend* Lady Meerka about this shabby treatment.

But it would be worth it. He'd solved a case. All by himself.

Can't wait to tell the guys about this at the Chain tonight. And maybe I'll get to tell Lieutenant Tresyllione, too. . . .

Five

"Tresyllione, ban Wyvald, my office!"

Torin looked at Danthres with bleary eyes as they hung their cloaks on the wall pegs. The words that echoed throughout the squad room came from Osric, who was standing in the doorway to the east-wall door. His stubble had grown in a bit, and his perpetual scowl was now deep enough to be visible on the back of his head.

Casting a longing glance at the pantry—he'd been hoping for some food, since he hadn't eaten anything in hours—Torin trudged toward the captain's office, Danthres right alongside him.

They had come in together after catching a couple of hours' sleep at Torin's apartment, the location of that sleep determined solely by virtue of it being closer to the Dog and Duck than Danthres's. Mercifully, the couple downstairs remained quiet—whether due to fear of Torin's wrath or a pause in their endless battle, Torin neither knew nor cared.

When the detectives entered the office, Osric was sitting in his chair. Torin found that he wasn't in the least bit encouraged by the fact that the captain wasn't sharpening his dagger. Based on the expression on his face, Torin fully expected flames to come shooting out of his good eye.

"Do you know what I had to do this morning?"

"Compose an honor guard for Sir Rommett to escort the remaining members of Brightblade's party to—"

Osric waved a hand at Torin. "After that. First I had to sit and listen to the chamberlain carry on at great length on the subject of you, Tresyllione."

"Sir," Danthres began.

"Shut up, Tresyllione, I don't want to hear it. Right now, you still have a job. The reason why you still have a job is because I told Sir Rommett that you would offer a full apology for your appalling behavior."

Danthres's eyes widened. "Apology? That jackass barged into the middle of an interrogation!"

"He's the chamberlain, Tresyllione, he can barge in wherever he wants."

"No, sir, he can't—the law clearly states that the investigating officer has supreme authority at a crime scene, and—"

Osric slammed his fist down on the desk, which startled the sleep-deprived Torin enough to make him almost fall out of his chair. He hadn't seen Osric let loose with such a display since the old days on the elven front. "Dammit, Tresyllione, you've been working here for over ten years, you should know better than to think that the rules actually apply to anyone who has the word *sir* in front of his name!"

"How are we supposed to question someone if the chamberlain's going to just take him away and hole him up in the castle?"

"Danthres," Torin said, trying to make it a warning.

"Listen to your own words, Tresyllione. *They're in the castle.* That means you have easy access to them any time you want, and they aren't going anywhere. Yes, it's for their protection as much as anything, but it also means that Ubàrlig, Brother Genero, those two halflings, and their barbarian friend are all right here where you can talk to them any time you want."

Looking down at her feet, Danthres muttered something.

"What was that, Tresyllione? I didn't hear you," Osric asked angrily.

"I said, I hadn't thought of that."

"Of course you hadn't. After all, you're only a detective, it's not like thinking is something that's expected of you."

Sarcasm now, Torin thought. *He really* is *furious.*

Fixing his one-eyed gaze so firmly on Danthres that Torin half-expected to see a hole appear in her forehead, Osric continued: "Now, when we're done here, you're going to go to Sir Rommett, and you're going to apologize. It will be a sincere and groveling apology. You will continue to apologize until such a time as Sir Rommett believes and accepts it. Failure to do so will result in your immediate termination, which would be bad for everyone, as I doubt that ban Wyvald will be able to solve this without you."

Torin blinked. "Wait a moment!"

"Shut up, ban Wyvald," Osric said without even looking at him. "Now then, what did you learn last night?"

"Well," Torin said, "Boneen finally showed up after we sent someone to drag him over. The results were the same as Brightblade's: His neck snapped from no apparent cause. In this case, it happened while he was composing a letter to someone named Efthran. No evidence of magic of any kind—nor any of a murderer. The dwarf found the body when he came up to fetch him for dinner with him and Brother Genero. He claimed the door was unlocked, but that's hardly unusual, all things considered. According to Ubàrlig, Olthar never outgrew that particular elven habit."

"Any other witnesses?"

Torin shook his head. "Last person to see him alive was an old man staying at the inn who saw him go upstairs to his room, then later saw Ubàrlig go up after him."

"Before Rommett blundered in," Danthres added, "the dwarf threw a ridiculous theory at us."

"Actually, it wasn't that ridiculous," Torin said. "Both Brightblade and lothSirhans were particular enemies of the Elf Queen."

Osric snorted. "An attack from beyond the grave?"

"Unlikely, given the lack of magic," Torin said. "But she prompted fierce loyalty in her people. There's the possibility that one of her devotees wants revenge. At the very least, we should have Dragon round up any elves in the area so we can talk to them."

Nodding, Osric said, "All right, I'll have Grint do a sweep. You can talk to them at Dragon—by the time Tresyllione's done with her apology, they should've gathered up at least enough for you to get started." Then he turned his fierce gaze on Torin. "Tell me that isn't all you have."

"No, we still have the others and the real reason why they're in Cliff's End."

"Which," Danthres said, "is the lead we should be pursuing instead of chasing elves around."

"I fought against the Elf Queen's troops, Tresyllione," Osric said. "I wouldn't put it past one of those fanatics to go after Brightblade and especially lothSirhans. Besides, if that's a lead that Ubàrlig gave you, then you *will* pursue it."

"Why?" Danthres asked. She had, Torin noticed, regained her acerbic tone, as if Osric had never read her the riot act. "We know that they're trying to deflect us. This is obviously part of that."

"Because, Tresyllione," Osric said slowly, "they're

staying in the castle as the guests of Lord Albin and Lady Meerka. *You* remember Lord Albin and Lady Meerka—they run the place. They're also pissed off that Olthar lothSirhans died in their city-state under mysterious circumstances. After getting one ear filled with Sir Rommett's bitching and moaning about the thuggish behavior of my lieutenants, the other ear was then filled with more bitching and moaning from Lord Albin about letting war heroes die on my watch." He leaned forward again. "The only thing I want filling my ears from now on is you two telling me how far you're coming with the case."

"You won't get that as long as we're wasting time with this 'lead' of Ubàrlig's."

"Perhaps, but the Lord and Lady *will* view it as progress, which is what matters at the moment. Besides, I think it's best that both of you stay away from that group until tomorrow. Give Sir Rommett a chance to cool down."

"So we're supposed to let our only real witnesses sit for two days, while—"

Osric leaned back again. "They're not going anywhere, Tresyllione. If they are conspiring, you'll have your shot at them tomorrow. If they're being targeted, they're safer in the castle than they would be at the Dog and Duck."

Torin put a hand on Danthres's shoulder before she could speak further. "We'll talk to the elves this afternoon, sir." He stood up. "Come on, Danthres, let's get to work."

"No, ban Wyvald, *you'll* get to work. Tresyllione's on her way to meet with Sir Rommett."

Through clenched teeth, Danthres said, "No, I'm not."

Osric spoke in a low, quiet, menacing tone. "I beg your pardon?"

"I said I'm not. I will not apologize to that imbecile. If it costs me my job, so be it." With that, she got up and left Osric's office.

The captain turned to Torin. "Ban Wyvald—"

Holding up a hand, Torin said, "I know, I know, I'll talk her into it." He got up and looked at the door. "Somehow."

He found Danthres gathering up some material on her desk. Aside from the pair of them, the squad room was empty. Dru, Hawk, Iaian, and Grovis were all out, presumably following leads in their own cases.

Torin stared at her from his side of their desk for several seconds. "So this is it? After ten years, you're just going to abandon the job because you don't want to make an apology?"

"Looks that way, doesn't it?"

"Why?"

"Because I won't let bastards like Rommett win."

Torin slammed his hand down on the desk. "It's not a battle, Danthres!"

Pursing her lips, Danthres asked, "Isn't it?"

"Unlike you, I've actually *been* a soldier. Trust me, this isn't war—this is politics."

"There's a difference?"

"Yes." Torin smiled. "Wars have more clearly defined rules. But in politics, you can't treat everyone as if they're an enemy the way you *always* do."

"I don't always do that."

"Yes, you do. You go into *every* situation with your sword up, whether or not you actually need it. The problem with that is, it usually just forces other people's hands and they take out their sword when they might not otherwise."

"And why not? It saves time. All my life, Torin, I've had to deal with people who think I'm an abomination at best. When I left Sorlin, I discovered just how rare it was for someone of my particular parentage to live beyond the age of one day. I came here—"

"You came here because Cliff's End isn't like that," Torin said. "I know all this already."

Danthres let out a long breath. "Then you should also know why I won't put up with shit from people like Rommett."

"What I know, Danthres, is that you've been living here for a decade. Isn't it time you lowered your sword at least once to someone other than me?"

"My way is safer."

"You're about to lose your *job,* Danthres. How is that 'safer'?"

Danthres snarled. "Better that than to turn into a smiling, naïve idiot like—" She cut herself off.

Torin walked over to her and looked her straight in the eye. "Like me? I thought *you* knew *me* better than that."

She stared into his eyes for several seconds before looking away. Torin was grateful to see that she at least had the good graces to look abashed. "You're a good man, Torin ban Wyvald," she said, "and remarkably good-natured for someone who's lived the life you've lived. But sometimes I think you're still too much the philosopher and not enough the soldier." Again, she faced him. "I wish I could live as you do, Torin, truly I do, but the world isn't populated by people like you, or even Osric. There are many more Rommetts and Grovises and Nultis and Manfreds."

Torin frowned. "Manfred?"

She shook her head. "That one at the Chain last night who thought I was 'exotic.' "

"Oh, him." Torin grinned. "Well, he's right, you *are* exotic. And I think I know that particular guard—he's one of the good ones. He's working Unicorn, and if he's the one I'm thinking of, Arron's grooming him for a promotion. Has the makings of a detective."

"Great. He can be your new partner, then. You'll get more respect from everyone else now that you're not partnered up with the ugly bitch."

Torin shook his head. "Funny. You've always told me that you don't give a damn about anything but justice, and seeing the right thing done."

"Exactly. There's no 'right' in whining for an apology to an aristocratic—"

"What about Gan Brightblade? And Olthar loth-Sirhans?"

"What *about* them? Their own friends don't seem to give a troll's ass whether or not we find their killer."

"So you don't, either?" Torin grabbed her by the shoulders. "I don't believe that. I don't believe that you would walk away from this just because your pride is hurt. Do you know why I don't believe it?"

"No," she muttered, "but I believe you'll tell me."

"Because that's what Sir Rommett would do."

That got her attention and she looked him in the eyes again. "What?"

"What you're doing now is exactly what politicians like Sir Rommett do—choose the way that saves face over the way that does the right thing. Apologizing to him won't cost you anything. You don't even have to *mean* it—his kind is easily taken in by shallow flattery, and I'm sure any flattery you provide will be shallow indeed."

Danthres barked a laugh at that, one that Torin knew was all but involuntary.

"It will get the job done, though. How many times have you said that the main thing we do here is speak for those who can't speak for themselves? Well, Brightblade and lothSirhans need *both* of us to speak for them."

Torin stared intently into Danthres's gray eyes.

The half-elf inhaled deeply through her nose, then let out a long breath through her mouth.

Finally, she said, "All right. I suppose I can give it a try. Besides," she added with a small smile, "Osric's right, you'll never solve this without me."

As Danthres turned and headed toward the west-wall doorway, Torin just shook his head. He then spoke to Jonas, who would deal with Dragon on getting the local elf population rounded up. The more Torin thought about it, the more he shared Danthres's feeling that this was probably a waste of time, but it was also good to eliminate the possibility.

When he was done giving those instructions to Jonas, the sergeant looked after the door through which Danthres had left. "How do you do it?"

"Do what?"

"Put up with her."

Torin shrugged. "Years of practice."

"How'd you do it ten years ago?"

This time he grinned. "Osric made it clear that partnering with her was the only way I'd get to join the Guard. Just as he made it clear to her that partnering with me was the only way she'd get to *stay* with the Guard. She'd already gone through seven partners in six months when I signed on."

"Not surprising, that." Jonas shook his head. "I'll get right on this, Lieutenant."

"Thank you, Jonas."

Once the sergeant left, and with Danthres gone,

the squad room was again empty, save for him. Torin sighed. He had been hoping to use one of the other detectives as a sounding board—especially Iaian, whose years of experience often aided in the thought process.

Torin thought back over the statements he'd gotten from the few witnesses to both murders, but came up more or less empty. The chambermaid who found Brightblade just filled in details of what they were able to reconstruct on their own. The people who saw them carousing at dinner the night before didn't give any indications that anyone there had been sufficiently put out to commit murder—certainly not a murder as elaborate as this.

What drove Torin craziest was the total lack of any kind of evidence turned up by the M.E. Normally, a case like this would have been put down already, by virtue of Boneen providing a description of the murderer—or, at the very least, there'd be sufficient evidence of magic that the case would be kicked over to the Brotherhood for *them* to deal with. Not always satisfying, but at least it didn't leave Torin and Danthres with a perpetually open case. Osric hated those, as they made the Guard look bad in the eyes of Lord Albin and Lady Meerka.

Instead, they had a genuine mystery, one complete with major political hassles guaranteed to make their lives more complicated.

At least we got the unlimited overtime.

A member of the youth squad came in then. Torin recognized her as one of the kids who worked the docks. After Torin provided the girl with a copper, she gave a message that no one matching the descriptions of any of Brightblade's party had been seen on the docks. *So they really hadn't gotten to the hiring part yet, nor have they since Brightblade's death.* He had been hoping for some revelation about their journey from a more impartial source than the party members themselves.

That left them with damn little—less for lothSirhans, owing to their incomplete interrogation of the person who found the body. The only other witness was that old man. . . .

Frowning, he thought back over the witnesses he'd talked to after Brightblade's murder. The old man who claimed to have seen lothSirhans going upstairs to his room was probably related to one of the younger men who told Torin about the revelry the night before Brightblade's murder.

Just then, a guard came in with a parchment. "Lieutenant, this just came for you—from the Dog and Duck."

Torin looked up to see that the fresh-faced young man was delivering the guest list, copied from the register by Olaf. Torin perused it, looking for any male-male combinations with the same family name. None came up—not that that meant anything in and of itself. They might not have used family names, they might have had different ones due to marriage. *Or you're just letting your imagination run away with you,* he chided himself. *Focus on the case, Torin, not the irrelevant side issues.*

Of course, that would be easier if the case itself weren't so maddening.

Jonas came in then, holding a much smaller piece of parchment. "One of the youth squad dropped this off at the gate."

Taking the parchment, Torin smiled. Some of the youth squad didn't like to set foot in headquarters. Bad luck, they thought, though it decreased their chances of getting their usual copper-piece tip. Unfolding the parchment, Torin saw that it was written in Old Myverin, and simply had the words "Come see me." It was unsigned, but the writer of the note hardly needed to sign—her handwriting was quite distinctive, and she was likely the only person besides Torin outside of Myverin's borders who could write in the old tongue in any case.

Informing Jonas that he'd be in Goblin for a while talking to an informant and asking him to let Danthres know that he'd meet her at Dragon Precinct later, Torin grabbed his cloak and proceeded to the seedier part of town.

Meerka Way—the primary thoroughfare, which led one from the castle to the Docklands—was always packed with people, but it provided the most direct route to Torin's destination. As he went, the mansions gave way to large houses, then smaller houses, then even smaller houses more crowded together, then shoved-together structures, culminating in the chaos that was the center of Cliff's End, at the border between Dragon and Goblin. The quality of the construction was in inverse proportion to the quantity of it per square foot.

The smell got worse as well. In Unicorn, his nose mostly detected foliage, some of it freshly cut and groomed. On this warm day in particular, it reminded him of the manors of Myverin, though how much of that was due to the note he'd received he wasn't sure. The farther into Cliff's End he progressed, the ranker the aroma became, from the less-well-hidden cesspools, to the poorer kitchens, to the less-well-groomed citizenry.

How that citizenry reacted to his presence altered as he went as well. In Unicorn, he was often greeted, sometimes warmly, but at least always politely, as if his presence were appreciated. In Dragon, the greetings were fewer and more guarded. By the time he crossed Axe Lane, the official demarcation point between Dragon and Goblin, few would look him in the eye, and those who did were either utterly contemptuous or scared.

No one batted an eyelash when he turned down Sandy Brook Way. Guards were often known to head that way, ostensibly to make arrests, but usually for pleasure. Prostitution was legal in Cliff's End—Lord Albin and Lady Meerka had never seen any good reason for selling sex to be against the law—but whorehouses were often used as fronts for shadier activities, and most of the best (and worst) whorehouses in Cliff's End were on Sandy Brook.

Torin passed several structures advertising assorted forms of negotiable sexual activities, some with the potential sex partner in question hawking the wares in front of the door. One establishment guaranteed that no glamours were used on their women, an assertion belied by the perfection of the woman standing in front of the door. *Perhaps,* he thought with a smile, *it would be more accurate to say that no* decent *glamours are used. . . .* A good glamour looked perfectly natural, of course, but good glamours were also very expensive.

At the cul-de-sac following the intersection of Sandy Brook and Doila Lane sat Torin's destination: Suzett's. The place was quiet and unassuming, only a small sign in the front window identifying the name of the establishment. Constructed primarily of dark wood, the place could easily be mistaken for one of the middle-class houses in Dragon. Suzett's women generally didn't use glamours, because they didn't need to—she knew how to dress them and make them up in such a way that magic was not required. And in the seven years she'd been running the place, they had never been connected to any illegal activity, which made them just about unique.

When he stepped through the giant wooden

door, Torin found that the smells of rubbish, rotten food, unkempt living creatures, and their assorted waste products were replaced with a floral aroma that seemed to permeate the entire lobby. Curtains kept the sun out of the room, leaving the illumination to dozens of scented candles festooned about. Aside from the small desk in the back, the place was furnished entirely with couches and cushions, all in subdued solid colors, which matched the soothing dark wood of the walls. This entire place was designed to make one relax.

A tall elven woman wearing a small top over a large pair of breasts—the cloth barely covered her nipples—a small strip of cloth suspended from a belt across her narrow hips, and nothing else walked forward from the desk. This wasn't a bad glamour, all things considered—she looked just like an elf, except for the disproportionately large chest. Humans sometimes achieved that lack of symmetry, Torin knew, but elves never did. The glamour either made her look elven or made her breasts seem larger; given her occupation, the former was more likely.

"Can I help you, Guard?" she asked, voice smooth as any elf's.

"Lieutenant, actually," Torin said with a smile. "I'm here to see Suzett."

"Do you have an appointment?"

From behind him, a voice that was even smoother, though it came from a human, said, "Lieutenant ban Wyvald needs no appointment to see me, Elshra."

Torin turned to see the unusually tall form of Suzett herself. She wore a blue silk gown with a scoop neck to accentuate her cleavage, and just enough makeup to highlight her soft features and cover up the very few lines and wrinkles that age had at last started to slice into her smooth skin. Her thick black hair fell loosely about her shoulders.

"One could argue that I *do* have an appointment," Torin said, removing the parchment from his belt. "You did send for me, after all."

Suzett's mouth had never, in all the years Torin had known her, formed a smile, yet her eyes would sometimes sparkle with amusement. They did so now. "True. Come with me."

She walked into the back room through a doorway covered in strings of beads that clacked slightly as she went through. The larger Torin with his leather armor and cloak made considerably more noise as he followed her through the beads.

This room had none of the peaceful qualities of the entry room—it was all parchments, scrolls on shelves, and a cluttered desk. This was where Suzett did the behind-the-scenes work that allowed her establishment to run smoothly. Torin was likely the only nonemployee who ever saw this part of the place.

"Elshra?" he asked as they entered the room. "What's her real name?"

"Does it matter? To the customers, she is a woman with an elven face and a human body—that is the greatest sexual desire of about half the men and a quarter of the women in this city."

"If you say so."

"I understand that you're investigating the deaths of Gan Brightblade and Olthar lothSirhans," Suzett said as she sat at the desk.

Torin took a seat in the wooden guest chair, which creaked from his weight, compounded by the armor and sword he carried. He suspected that the chair was chosen with lithe women in mind. Neutrally, he said, "Word travels fast." In truth he would have been amazed if Suzett didn't know he and Danthres were the investigating officers before they themselves knew.

"Many words have traveled to me, my sweet lieutenant. Including a report that your magical examiner found no traces of sorcery."

Torin raised his eyebrows. "And how did you come by *that* information?"

Suzett's eyes sparkled again. "Do you really expect me to answer that?"

"No, but I still had to ask."

"Well, the reason why this surprised me is that dear Gan—" Suzett hesitated. "I've known Gan for quite some time, from back in the days before I was a successful entrepreneur."

Laughing, Torin said, "I've known you as far more than an entrepreneur, Suzett."

"True. And if anyone else were investigating this murder, I would never share this information, but since I do owe you . . ."

"Suzett, you do not have to justify yourself to me. If you have information, please provide it."

She shook her head. "Always straight to the point, aren't you, Lieutenant?"

"It *is* part of the job description. A fact of which you should be aware, given what happened eight years ago."

Now the sparkle left her eyes altogether. Torin knew she did not like being reminded of the events that led to her status as one of his best informants—and also his only unpaid one.

"Gan used a glamour potion."

Torin frowned. "That's not possible. Boneen would have detected that. He must have stopped using it."

"I saw him two days ago when he and his friends checked into the Dog and Duck."

At that, Torin smiled. "What were *you* doing in the Dog and Duck?" Suzett rarely ventured outside her place.

"I had business—an itinerant barber who did not perform his tonsorial services after payment was rendered."

Torin shook his head. Suzett usually didn't fall for such scams. "Bad day?"

"My day off, actually." Her lovely, porcelain face grew hard. "It is the last time I will leave Cosra in charge." Then her features softened. "In any case, the glamour was still in full effect when I laid eyes upon him. His eyes were clear, his hair solid brown, his face unlined, just as it was when I first met him."

"He used a potion, you say—not a gem?"

Suzett shook her head. "A potion. He said he didn't trust gems, and he could afford the potions—especially given how many wizards he was friends with."

Torin scratched his beard. "That is useful." *I'm not sure how yet, but it is.* He rose. "Is there anything else?"

"Are you still partnered with that half-elven creature?"

"Her name is Danthres."

"She's a horrible woman, my sweet lieutenant. You should find yourself someone more pleasant."

"Danthres can be quite pleasant."

"When she's asleep, perhaps. I've never met anyone so embittered."

"She comes by it naturally. Unlike your Elshra out there, she is *naturally* half-elf and half-human, and that comes with a price in the real world."

Once more, Suzett's eyes sparkled, even as she rose from her chair. "Then perhaps she should indulge in a fantasy world a bit more often."

Torin laughed again. "I'll pass that on to her." He walked toward the beads. "Thank you, Suzett."

"You have no need to thank me, my sweet lieutenant, ever, for anything. You know that I am forever in your debt." Her lips did curl slightly, and she leaned forward, making sure that Torin could see her cleavage quite clearly. "Another man would take more advantage of that."

"Good thing I'm not another man, then." Torin grinned and left.

As he headed back down Sandy Brook toward Meerka Way, he pondered both Suzett's body and her oh-so-tempting offer, as well as the cleaning woman at the Dog and Duck, and what she said about Gan Brightblade's appearance when his body had been discovered.

Apologizing to Sir Rommett took Danthres about two hours, which proved Torin wrong. He had said it would cost her nothing, but in fact it cost her two hours of her life. Still, the shit-brained aristocrat accepted the apology and lectured her for an hour about any number of things that Danthres could not recall by virtue of not having paid any attention to him. She departed his rather posh office in the western wing of the castle as the possessor of both her job and one of her worst moods in recent memory. More than anything, she felt the urge to strangle a small, defenseless animal.

Upon her return to the squad room, Jonas informed her that Torin had hied off to Goblin to talk to an informant—probably that simpering bitch who ran the whorehouse. Danthres decided that the animal didn't necessarily need to be defenseless.

She proceeded down Meerka Way to Dragon Precinct to begin the fruitless interrogation of local elves, in the hopes that one of them might be a secret devotee of the Elf Queen, a prospect she considered about as likely as one of them being King Marcus in disguise.

When she arrived, Sergeant Grint informed her that Torin had not arrived yet, but they'd rounded up about a score of elves, with a few more to come, and she could use the interrogation room.

After the first few—with no sign of Torin to relieve and/or assist her—she would happily have strangled an entire horde of small animals, defenseless or otherwise.

"I am afraid I do not know that of which you speak."

"You don't know who Olthar lothSirhans is?"

"Oh, yes, I know of him. Who does not?"

"Did you know that he was in Cliff's End?"

"Where?"

"Cliff's End."

"Where is that?"

"You're *in* Cliff's End."

"Oh, is *that* the name of this city? I didn't realize."

"Have you ever met Olthar lothSirhans?"

"Goodness, no. Though I might, if you say he's here in Cliff's End."

When she gave up and tossed that one out of the interrogation room, the next spoke in Ra-Telvish. "This will be brief. I have better things to do—"

In Common, Danthres said, "This is a murder investigation."

Still speaking Ra-Telvish, the man said, "Then you should be finding the murderer."

"Speak Common, please."

"If you do not understand my words, you ignorant half-breed slut, that is your problem, not mine. I do not speak the gutter language of lower life-forms such as humans." The man folded his arms defiantly.

Danthres gave him her best don't-piss-me-off-or-I'll-kill-you smile. "I understood every word you said," she said in her slightly accented Ra-Telvish, "but I prefer not to speak the arrogant, irritating language of lower life-forms such as elves." Back to Common: "Now then, did you know Olthar loth-Sirhans?"

He did not. Neither did the next few. The one after that went on at great length at the injustice of the man who "saved us all from the Bitch Queen," and proclaimed that she would personally pay for Olthar's funeral, and make sure he went to the next life with the highest honors.

Danthres concluded that interview by assuring her that such arrangements were likely being taken care of.

By the time she hit a dozen—and an elf who had several unkind words regarding Danthres's parentage and face—Torin finally deigned to turn up.

"Where the hell've *you* been?" She shook her

head. "Never mind, I don't know and I don't care. You can take the next batch of these tiresome, insufferable—"

"No need," Torin said with a grin as he perched on the table in the interrogation room. "I had Grint send the rest home. He said you weren't getting anywhere, and I think we've done enough to keep up appearances for the sake of our Lord and Lady. Besides, I have something a bit better."

Danthres bit back an angry retort at Torin's words, instead clinging to his last sentence like a drowning victim being thrown a life preserver. "A lead?"

"The beginnings of one." He proceeded to tell her what he'd learned about Brightblade's use of a glamour potion. "The potion would stop working when he died," he finished, "but the magical residue from a potion lasts until the body decomposes—sometimes even after that. There's no way Boneen could've missed that."

"How reliable is your source?"

He smirked. "Suzett has never led me astray before."

Danthres sighed. "I had a feeling it was her. You *do* know she's just trying to get into your armor."

"That's not quite how our relationship works."

"I can imagine," Danthres said with a snort. "I don't like her."

"That's hardly indicative of anything suspicious. You don't like anybody."

Danthres got up and started pacing the room. "She's a whore, Torin. For all we know she was paid by one of Brightblade's friends to give us this false lead."

"She's been my best informant for eight years, Danthres," Torin said emphatically. "I doubt she's going to start lying to me now. And her story does match what the cleaning woman said about his looking grayer and more wrinkled after he died."

"That could've been the light."

Torin nodded. "Or it could've been a proper observation. Remember, all the tavern was trying to get a look at Brightblade. They probably spent most of the evening staring at him. If they thought he looked different—especially if he didn't match the picture they had of him from the previous night—we have to consider the possibility that he actually *did* look different."

"We still don't know that it was a potion."

"Suzett seemed to think it—"

Danthres turned to glare at her partner. "When was the last time your precious whore saw Brightblade before seeing him at the Dog and Duck?"

"She didn't say."

Typical, Danthres thought. *He's letting that woman impair his judgment.* "What if it's been a few years? Perhaps in his old age he couldn't afford the potions anymore and stuck with a gem."

"Which we didn't find on his person or in his room."

"The murderer could've taken it."

"What murderer? Boneen didn't see one. Nor did he see any evidence of magic." Torin blew out a breath. "You see what I mean about this being the beginnings of a lead. I'm not sure what this means, but it *does* mean something."

"It could just mean that the whore is leading you by your nether regions."

Before they could pursue this conversation any further, the door to the interrogation room opened to reveal Sergeant Grint. Grint was tall and broad-shouldered, and his leathery face bore the forty years he'd served the Guard in every deep crag and wrinkle. Even his bald pate had wrinkles, weaving in and out amid the blue veins that seemed to throb near the surface of his scalp. "Got somethin' for ya," he said in his sandpapery voice, "but y'ain't gonna like it."

"What?" Danthres asked.

"Gotcha 'nother coupla bodies."

"We're on a case," Torin said.

"I *know* that, y'idjit," Grint snapped. "S'part of it. Two halflings, no waitin'." He snickered. "Found 'em down Jorbin's Way. Guard recognized 'em from the Dog and Duck."

Danthres put her head in her hands. "Mari and Nari?"

"Looks like. Figured you two'd wanna check it out."

"Good figuring." Torin then looked at Danthres.

"Wasn't the whole point of the exercise to keep them *in* the castle?"

Danthres's only reply was to leave the room. This case just got even more peculiar, and the only good thing was that the overtime was probably going to last a little longer.

Hobart lit a cigar as he stood at the mouth of Jorbin's Way, waiting to be able to get back to his stand. The center of much of Cliff's End's mercantile commerce, Jorbin's Way was lined with various stands and establishments that sold pretty much anything in the way of material goods you could possibly want. Hobart mostly dealt in dry goods—clothes, tools, and other items that were easy to store without magical aid. He saw no reason to pay the exorbitant fees that the Brotherhood of Wizards insisted on for spells to preserve food, drink, and certain other substances. He preferred to stick with what he could place in a box and shove in a closet if need be. Particularly those items that were of dubious legality.

Right now, Hobart was exceedingly grateful that he had no such goods in his booths, as the damned Swords had shut the Way down and were crawling all over everything ever since those two halflings dropped dead. The last thing he needed was some overzealous Sword going through his stand and finding the stash of Iaron tobacco that he hadn't actually paid any tariffs on, or those rubies that he had labeled as genuine pieces of the famed Eye of Magril.

If there was any good news to be had, it was that they picked today. With both Gan Brightblade and Olthar lothSirhans dying in Cliff's End within a day of each other, people weren't in particularly good humor, which meant they weren't especially interested in buying things. Hobart had been hearing a great deal of moaning and weeping over the kind of world we live in where heroes can die, and a concomitant lack of discussion over what to get for that wedding next month or for a family member's birthday. Profits were lower today than they'd been since winter. Having the Way shut down was, in its own way, the perfect ending to a perfect day.

As if this enforced exile weren't taking long enough, a couple more Swords approached from Meerka escorting two more Swords through. One Sword pushed Hobart out of his path hard enough to knock his cigar to the ground. *Ain't touching that now, I* know *where that ground has been. Too bad, those Barlin stogies ain't cheap.*

The new Swords that came through wore brown cloaks. *Oh for Temisa's sake, not detectives,* he thought, pulling out another cigar. *Now we're gonna be here for* hours.

One of them stopped and looked right at Hobart. *Oh, shit. Not her.*

"Well well well," Lieutenant Tresyllione said. "If it

isn't Hobart. Why is it that every time I come to the Way to investigate something, you're right in the thick of it?"

" 'Sall my bad luck," Hobart said sourly, blowing out a puff of smoke. " 'Salways my bad luck whenever yer 'round, Lieutenant."

"Maybe. Right now, it's the bad luck of the halflings that I'm concerned with. I'll be back."

"Mind hurryin' up? Fella's gotta make an honest livin'—"

"Hobart, you haven't made an honest living a day in your life."

Letting the slander pass, Hobart went on. "—an' I can't be doin' that if'n you Swords're keepin' our businesses shut."

One of the guards leaned over. "Watch your mouth, Hobart."

Tresyllione's partner waved the guard off. "It's all right," ban Wyvald said. "He's entitled to express his dismay with the current situation."

"Yeah, well, I'm feelin' a whole lotta dismay, truth be known." Hobart took a long drag on his cigar. "Look, them two halflings died'n that's a pity, it surely is. But we been coolin' our boots out here f'r an hour, an' now we gotta wait for you Cloaks t'get through what you gotta do."

"That's right," Tresyllione said, "we do. If you have a problem with that, you can complain to your local representative. I believe that it's Shramian for this district." She smiled, which actually made her look scarier. "I'm sure you know where to find him, Hobart, it's where you send the bribes."

"Now that's just a damn lie." Strictly speaking, it was. Hobart's bribes to Shramian went through a middle party.

"But it won't do any good." Tresyllione looked around at the assembled merchants. Her partner went ahead, probably to check the bodies, but she stayed behind and continued talking. "See, those halflings that died are close personal friends of Lord Albin and Lady Meerka. We're going to need to be quite thorough in our investigation. So we could be here for *hours*. Probably the rest of the day, to be honest. I wouldn't count on opening again until tomorrow morning—or even noontime."

Half a dozen complaints, groans, and moans sounded from the other merchants around Hobart at that. Hobart, however, was not among them. He'd known Tresyllione since she was walking a beat in Goblin. She wouldn't have wasted her time with that explanation normally; she wouldn't care enough, truth be told, she'd just keep the Way closed until she was done. No, she only spelled it out because she wanted something in exchange for possibly shortening the time that the Way would be shut down.

Never let it be said I passed up an opportunity. "Look, Lieutenant, I've always been a personable sort toward the Guard."

"No you haven't."

Hobart shrugged. "All right, maybe I haven't, but it ain't too late to start, is it? I'm thinkin' it's time I turned over a new leaf. After all, we're all on the same side, ain't we? We just want law an' order in our little town here."

"No, Hobart, *I* want law and order. You want a high profit margin, and you see a big one by helping out with the murder investigation of a close personal friend of the Lord and Lady."

Hobart shook his head. "Y'know, it do just depress me, the cynicism you see nowadays. Here I am, tryin' t'be civic-minded an' all, and you insult me."

"I'm not insulting you, Hobart, I'm describing you." She walked up to him, towering over him. *Women shouldn't be so damn tall,* he thought irritably. "But that doesn't mean I won't accept your offer, regardless of your motives. Did you see anything?"

Letting the question hang for a moment, Hobart took a final drag of his cigar, which was now down to almost a nub. He dropped it on the ground, stepped on it, and finally said, "Shit, Lieutenant, I saw the whole damn thing. Them two halflings was runnin' their scam right in front'a my place. First they came up an' asked me if'n I had any Cormese silk." He chuckled as he pulled out another cigar. "They took one look at my bolts'n gave me a price that was—well, pretty danged insultin'. Wouldn't give my own grandmother one copper per foot for Cormese silk."

"As I recall from the last time I wandered down the Way," Tresyllione said with a smirk, "what you generally refer to as 'Cormese silk' is in fact Hymian burlap, which tends to disintegrate when you wash it, and is also worth about a copper piece per foot."

"Y'see," Hobart said, throwing up his hands in frustration, "it's just this kinda thing that makes dealin' with you Cloaks such a pain in my ass."

"You'll get over it. What happened then?"

"Look, anyone who tries to wash Cormese silk deserves what they get, dammit. I mean, what kinda world we live in when you won't even take the word of an honest merchant?"

Tresyllione favored him with her ugly smile again. "As soon as I meet an honest merchant, I'll ask him. What happened then? And don't make me ask a third time if you want to open again before harvest."

Hobart, in fact, had plenty more invective, but decided to save it; he remembered what Tresyllione was like when she got pissed off. "After they pawed through half my damn merchandise, they commenced to pullin' the sick-brother scam. Not bad, neither—they looked like clueless tourists tryin' t'scrape enough together to get to a healer, an' they *promise* t'pay back as *soon* as their uncle comes into town t'morrow mornin' on some ship'r other." Hobart laughed. "Gotta admit, I seen better, but I seen a lot worse, too, and they was pickin' on a coupla gnome tourists who didn't know their tiny asses from their gangly elbows. Now the halflings, they got themselves a couple silvers, an' were makin' arrangements with th'gnomes t'meet t'morrow t're-pay 'em when all of a sudden, boom!"

"Boom?" Tresyllione prompted.

Again, Hobart shrugged. "Boom. They jus' dropped dead outta nowhere. Damndest thing I ever saw. Them two gnomes, they ran faster'n shit—didn't think legs that small could move s'fast."

"Do you remember what the gnomes looked like?"

Hobart shrugged. "Short, big noses. Looked like gnomes."

Tresyllione let out a breath through her teeth. "Think, Hobart, they must have had *some* distinguishing characteristics."

Taking a thoughtful drag on his cigar, Hobart cast his mind back. Truth be told, he wasn't really paying much attention to the gnomes, as he was more interested in the halflings' technique. The marks were incidental; Hobart really needed to know if these two halflings were going to be providing any kind of significant competition.

Then he recalled one detail. "The woman, she had a mole on her left cheek 'bout the size of a copper."

Tresyllione looked over at one of the Swords, who just nodded and walked off. *Damn, it's like they have some kind of Thought Spell. Shit, maybe they* do. *Certainly would explain a helluva lot.*

"Anything else?"

"Ain't that enough?" Hobart asked indignantly.

"Depends on your definition of the word, doesn't it?" Danthres smiled insincerely. "Thanks for your help, Hobart. If you *do* decide to share anything else, let a guard know."

Hobart shook his head as the lieutenant turned and headed down the Way to join her partner. *Bitch,* he thought.

"Thanks very much for your assistance," Torin told the elderly man for the third time.

"Eh? What?" The man blinked. "What was that, again? My what?"

Torin sighed. "Thank you, sir."

"Oh, right, very good. Yes. You're welcome." Then the old man frowned. "For what, exactly?"

Again, Torin sighed. "Your assistance in our investigation."

"Oh, right. Yes. Indeed." The old man looked around. "I don't know this place."

"You're in Jorbin's Way," Torin said helpfully.

The old man shook his head and started wandering off.

Shaking his head, Torin turned to Danthres and Boneen, who were walking up behind him. They stood in the center of Jorbin's Way, right next to a dried-meat stand owned by an old woman who, if Torin recalled correctly, tended to mislabel her jerky. Boneen absently grabbed a sliver of something that was advertised as being from the finest breed of cattle in Velessa, but which Torin knew was in fact from the local goat population.

"Who was that?" Danthres asked.

"Witness. He said he saw the halflings drop dead while talking to a pair of gnomes. At least, he said that eventually. Poor old man's half-addled, but he did say that the female gnome had dirt on her left cheek."

Danthres nodded. "That more or less tracks with Hobart's mole. We've already got some guards looking for them."

"Good. And I'm glad we have Hobart for a witness—I'd rather not subject that old man to the magistrate if we can avoid it. It took him half an hour simply to remember what a gnome was. He's even worse than—" Torin cut himself off.

"What is it?" Danthres prompted.

"I just realized that the man I just talked to bore a striking resemblance to two other witnesses. Not the same man, obviously—he's about twenty years older than the second one and fifty years older than the first—but it is odd. That's three different people who have similar physical appearances."

"If you're *quite* finished with these irrelevancies," Boneen said irritably while chewing on his dried goat meat, "I thought you might like to know what I found."

Torin grinned. "Let me guess—absolutely nothing?"

Scowling, Boneen said, "Yes. Same as Brightblade

and lothSirhans. First one, then the other fell down without any outside agency helping them along. No evidence of magic of any kind."

"You should examine these bodies carefully then," Torin said. "I've never known a grifter who didn't have *some* kind of magic on them. It's almost part of the job description."

"Definitely," Danthres said. "Hobart said they were moderately talented, which means they were probably very good and he just wouldn't admit it."

"Oh, that's just what I need, *more* work." Boneen took another bite of jerky. "Bad enough that Albin and Meerka keep sending their flunkies to hound me, now you want me examining halfling remains."

"If you're fishing for sympathy, you'll get nothing from us," Danthres said. "Those flunkies are tap-dancing on our spleens as well."

"The next one gets turned into a newt, I can tell you that. Hurry up and solve this damned case, will you? I haven't had a proper nap in days."

With that, Boneen muttered something, gestured four times, and then disappeared in a flash of light. Recognizing the sigils he was inscribing in the air, Torin had the foresight to shield his eyes. Some of the other nearby guards had less warning and blinked in annoyance at the residue of the teleport spell.

Danthres blinked a few times herself—her eyes were more sensitive, so even with the warning, she would, Torin knew, be seeing spots for the next several minutes. "Well, he'll get that nap now. Teleport Spells always make him woozy."

Torin scratched his beard. "I think we can reopen the Way. It'll keep the merchants happy, and there really isn't anything to be gained here. We know what happened, and we're no closer than before to finding out why."

"I want to talk to Genero and Ubàrlig—and the guards at the castle," Danthres added. "Those two shouldn't have been on the street in the first place, and I want to know why they were."

Torin agreed, and the pair of them walked back to the castle with the express purpose of doing just that.

By the time they arrived, the sun was beginning to set, and the time-chimes had long since rung nineteen. Torin yawned several dozen times on the walk back up Meerka Way. *When was the last time I slept? Oh, right, for two hours last night.* He sighed. *Unlimited overtime. Just remember that.*

Still, he found the walk through the crowded streets of Cliff's End to be draining, and wished he could have simply teleported back like Boneen.

"Look, Torin," Danthres started, then hesitated.

Torin frowned. "What?"

"I'm—I'm sorry about before. What I said about you, I mean."

In fact, Torin had already forgiven her, in part because he knew it was as much her anger talking as anything, and in part because he was self-aware enough to know that she wasn't entirely wrong. "Don't worry about it. This case has both of us irritable."

"It's not the case—I mean, it's not like we've never dealt with a big murder before, and it's not like we haven't dealt with shit from on high before."

"And it's not like you've ever been anything but testy and unpleasant," Torin said, deciding to be blunt and have done with it. "It's what makes you Danthres."

"Perhaps." She smiled. "But it might not be bad to be a little less Danthres."

"Well, wait until we close this case, because until we do, I need a complete Danthres."

She shook her head. "I'm not sure she'll do you any good. We've got four impossible murders with no evidence."

"We do have suspects, though, and it's past time we got answers out of them. I think our most sensible course would be to get the truth out of the remaining members of their little quest."

Danthres's face clouded over. "Long past time, yes."

When they arrived at the castle, they bypassed the eastern wing altogether. Instead, Danthres led the way to Sir Rommett's office; she knew the route well, having just gone there this morning.

As they approached, the officious-looking middle-aged man who sat at a small desk outside the oaken double doors that led to the chamberlain's sanctum sanctorum spoke without preamble. "I'm sorry, but the chamberlain is quite busy. I'm sure if you make an appointment, he will see you tomorrow."

"I'm afraid it cannot wait, good sir," Torin said, shooting Danthres a look to indicate that he would handle this his way instead of hers. The last time she'd been set loose on a castle official, it led to her first trip to Rommett's office, and Torin had no urge to repeat *that.*

"It will *have* to wait. The chamberlain is a *very* busy man." The secretary shuffled some parchments on his desk, having only spent a moment even bothering to look at the detectives. "As I said, you may make an appointment. However, as it is the end of the day, tomorrow is the earliest I can promise anything—and even at that, it is a risky proposition. He has a great deal of *important* work tomorrow."

"This is a murder investigation, good sir," Torin said through clenched teeth, now having a bit of a harder time keeping his pleasant bearing. Generally, he was better at this sort of thing, but the lack of sleep was impairing his abilities.

"I'm sure it's *very* important to the two of you, but the chamberlain has loftier concerns."

Oh, the hell with it. He glanced at Danthres, and gave her a look indicating that perhaps it was best to handle it her way.

She looked back at him and smiled. Then she leaned down, placing her fists on the desk. "You tell Sir Rommett that Lieutenants Tresyllione and ban

Wyvald are here to speak to him about our murder investigation. He'll want to speak to us, I think."

"As I keep explaining, the chamberlain is *quite* busy. Now if you—"

Danthres turned to one of the guards who stood at attention in the hallway. "Guard, do us a favor and please take this man away."

The secretary drew himself upright even as the guard walked over to join them. "I *beg* your pardon!"

Torin smiled sweetly. "You are impeding a murder investigation, good sir, and therefore are subject to arrest on the grounds of obstruction. Don't worry, the guard will take good care of you."

"Right this way, sir," the guard said, grabbing the secretary by his arm.

"No need to be gentle with him," Danthres said. "After all, he is standing in the way of the investigation into the deaths of the close personal friends of the Lord and Lady, so he's not especially worthy of respect."

With a grin, the guard said, "Not a problem, ma'am."

"Wait a minute, wait a minute!" The secretary, who had been lifted forcibly from his chair by the right arm, was turning quite pale. "I'm *sure* the chamberlain will see you. Just *please*, if you don't mind, give me just *one* second to speak with him, I'm *sure* that it can be worked out, just *please* don't take me down to the hole, I'll take care of it, *please*."

The guard looked at Danthres. "Ma'am?"

Danthres pretended to consider the matter. "Oh, very well," she said after a moment. "Let him make an attempt to salvage his situation."

As soon as the guard let go of his arm, the secretary bolted for the double doors, threw them open with a strength that belied his rail-thin form, and slammed them shut behind him.

"You enjoyed that, didn't you?" Torin asked.

"That?" Danthres snorted. "That was just the warm-up."

"If you need me again, sir, ma'am, I'll be *right* ovcr there," the guard said in a tone that indicated that he'd be more than happy to render aid once again. Torin suspected that being posted in proximity to the secretary had bred no small dcgree of contempt for the man.

The doors opened again to reveal the supercilious face of Sir Rommett. He stood with his hands on his hips in a gesture that probably did a wonderful job of intimidating the pageboys in the castle, but served only to make Torin want to burst out laughing. *This man wouldn't last half a second in Goblin.* Of course, he also had the power to order the ruination of any citizen in Goblin, so perhaps it was a fair tradeoff.

"Our apologies, good Sir Rommett, but I'm afraid that your secretary did not understand the urgency of the situation," Torin said. "We need to speak with you immediately."

"Can this not wait, Lieutenants?" Rommett asked

in a tone of great suffering. "I have a great deal of—"

Danthres, typically, got straight to the point. "Mari and Nari are dead."

Rommett's small mouth hung open in midword at that. "What? That's not possible! There are guards on their room!"

"Not especially talented ones, I'm afraid," Torin said. "The twins were murdered on Jorbin's Way."

"That's not possible," Rommett repeated.

"And yet it's true," Danthres said. "According to the M.E., they died the same way as Gan Brightblade and Olthar lothSirhans. Now, we need to speak to Brother Genero and General Ubàrlig and their barbarian friend right now—assuming, of course, that you haven't allowed *them* to leave the castle, either."

Rommett managed to go even paler than his secretary had. "This is terrible!"

"I daresay," Torin said dryly. "You have already obstructed and delayed this investigation, Sir Rommett, and now two more people are dead. We need to speak to what few witnesses we have remaining."

"Yes, of course," Rommett said distractedly. "Whatever you need. Bertram!"

The secretary poked his head out the door, but refused to step through it. "S-sir?"

"You are to help these two lieutenants in whatever way necessary. This simply *cannot* be allowed to continue."

"Especially," Danthres said with a vicious grin, "since the Lord and Lady no doubt made you personally responsible for the safety of Brother Genero and his friends. Or did you volunteer to be responsible? That would be even worse," she added thoughtfully.

"Please, Lieutenants," Rommett said as if Danthres had not spoken, "use whatever resources you need. Bertram here will aid you." The chamberlain turned around and walked back through the double doors, muttering, "This sort of thing *cannot* be permitted to happen."

Bertram oozed out from the doorway just as Rommett closed the doors behind him with a resounding thud.

"Er," Bertram said in a small voice, "shall I bring you to Brother Genero's chambers first, or to General Ubàrlig's?"

"Neither," Danthres said before Torin had a chance to answer. "Bring them and the barbarian to Sergeant Jonas in the eastern wing." She turned and left the hallway. Torin ran to catch up to her. Before he could ask, she said, "I want to talk to them on *our* terms this time, in *our* interrogation rooms."

As soon as they entered the squadroom, Osric emerged from his office. "Do you have good news for me?"

"Not yet," Torin said honestly, "but soon. We have some leads, and we're about to interrogate Genero, Ubàrlig, and Bogg."

Osric sputtered, "You're what? If Rommett finds out—"

"We have Rommett's full support," Danthres said a little too smugly.

"It seems," Torin added, "that the halflings' being killed on the streets of Cliff's End while they were supposed to be under the protection of the castle has Sir Rommett a bit unsettled."

"He's now our best friend in Flingaria," Danthres said.

At that, Osric actually smiled. "Good work. Keep me posted." Then he retreated to his office.

"Was that a smile?" Danthres asked.

"I believe it was, yes."

They passed Jonas on the way to their desk. He was shuffling parchments, as usual. "You two seen Dru or Hawk?"

Torin shook his head. "We just arrived ourselves. Why?"

"Someone in Dragon thinks they got a lead on their rapist."

"Wouldn't they have gone off shift by now?" Danthres asked.

Jonas shook his head. "They haven't checked out yet. Which is their tough shit, since they're not as lucky as some regarding overtime requests."

"Not everyone is fortunate enough to be us," Danthres said. "In a few minutes, a pale stringbean of a man will be bringing in a dwarf, a barbarian, and a Temisan priest. Put one in each room."

The sergeant nodded absently and continued shuffling his parchments. *It's a good thing I know*

Jonas, Torin thought with amusement, *since an objective observer would think he was ignoring us.*

To Danthres, he said, "You're in a good mood."

"After the way this day has gone, I'm looking forward to this."

"And you enjoyed sticking it to Rommett."

"Damn right. Especially after having to actually treat Hobart with something resembling respect."

"Hobart's not that bad."

"No, he's worse. But he gave us what we need. We just need to pull it together. And that's where our three friends will come in."

Torin was grateful to finally be using their own interrogation rooms instead of the ones at the precincts, or side rooms in the Dog and Duck. They were much better suited to the task: lit only by a single lantern, and containing three chairs and one small table. Rooms with little light and many shadows tended to make people nervous, and nervous people tended to be on the chatty side. Torin doubted that such simplistic techniques would work on combat veterans like these three, but he saw no reason not to take advantage of every possibility.

When Jonas informed them that each of the threesome had been placed in a room, Torin and Danthres then spent the next half an hour sitting at their desk comparing notes on what they were told by the witnesses at all three murders. It wasn't anything they hadn't discussed already at great length, but sometimes this sort of review bore fruit. It didn't in this case, but it did serve the dual purpose of having everything fresh in their minds, and also to frustrate their three witnesses by making them wait in a poorly lit room doing nothing for half an hour.

They decided to speak with Bogg first.

" 'Bout time!" he thundered as soon as they opened the door. The barbarian stood a full head taller than Danthres and his shoulders alone were twice as wide. He wore only a loincloth and a back scabbard for his sword. The scabbard was currently empty, as only the Guard was allowed to roam the halls of the castle armed. This relieved Torin, as he recalled the barbarian's sword as being almost as tall as Bogg himself. His comparative lack of clothing left his bronzed, heavily scarred skin on display for all to see, as well as the thick muscles in his chest, arms, and legs.

Bogg also smelled considerably better than he had two days ago. Torin suspected that the Lord and Lady insisted that Bogg make use of the castle's bathing facilities whether he wanted to or not.

" 'Nother minute, an' I was gonna break down the door. Then I was gonna break some heads. Then I was gonna get *mad*."

"Our apologies," Torin said gently, "but I'm afraid we had some paperwork to deal with, you understand."

"I don't understand shit. I just wanna know what I'm doin' in here."

"You do know that we're investigating the murders of—"

"Gan an' Olthar, yeah I know. So what?"

"And of Mari and Nari."

"Say what?"

"Mari and Nari," Torin said. "The halfling twins."

"Yeah, I *know* who they are, shitbrain. You mean t'tell me they're dead, too?"

"Yes," Torin said gravely. "They were killed at Jorbin's Way this morning."

Bogg slammed a massive fist onto the table, leaving a fist-sized impression in the wood and several splinters in the fist in question. Bogg didn't seem to notice the latter. "Who did it?"

"That's what we're trying—" Torin started.

" 'Cause I'm tellin' ya right now, I'm gonna kill 'em. I'm gonna kill 'em with my bare hands. None'a this turn-the-other-cheek crap that Genero's always spoutin', or justice instead'a revenge like Olthar usedta say. And I sure as shit ain't gonna settle for just cuttin' the guy's ear off, like that dumb kid outside'a town. Naw, I'm gonna grab 'em by the neck and then I'm gonna squeeze—"

"We're hoping it doesn't come to that," Torin said quickly.

"You know," Danthres said suddenly, "it's funny."

Bogg's face contorted and he raised his fists to chest level. "Funny? You think this is *funny,* you ugly bitch?"

"I'm not referring to the murder of your friends," she said in an unusually conciliatory manner.

"Good thing. 'Cause if you were makin' fun'a me—"

"I would never do that," Danthres lied. "No, I was talking about you."

That seemed to confuse Bogg; his fists lowered to his hips. "What about me?"

"Well, it's interesting to me. Brightblade was one of the great human heroes. In an odd sort of way, so was lothSirhans. And Ubàrlig has certainly made a name for himself, as has Brother Genero, if for no other reason than the uniqueness of one of his calling being at the forefront of Flingarian history."

Torin picked up the thread. "And then there's you. Until we met following Brightblade's murder, I had no idea who you were. The songs don't mention Bogg."

"I don't care about that kinda thing. Shit, neither did Mari or Nari."

Danthres shrugged. "They're halfling grifters—they live their lives in the shadows. Too much of the spotlight makes it harder for them to function. But not you. You're a lot more blunt."

Bogg moved menacingly toward Danthres. "What're you tryin' t'say t'me?"

Unsurprisingly, Danthres refused to be menaced. Boneen had magicked the entire castle so that no acts of person-on-person violence could be committed within its walls, so the detectives had nothing to fear from their interview subjects. "I'm not *trying* to say anything—but we have often found that you can sometimes trace the perpetrator of the crime to who has actual motivation to commit it."

"I have heard many songs sung about the heroism of Gan Brightblade and the bravery of Olthar loth-Sirhans," Torin added, "yet nothing about Bogg the Barbarian."

"Yeah, you *said* that already, redbeard," Bogg said, turning his bulk toward Torin, his fists poised as if to throw the mightiest punch imaginable, "an' you know what? I don't give a shit! Let Gan an' Olthar an' them have their shitty songs and their shitty painted women. *Real* men step up when it matters—an' that includes those two! Out there, we were the *best!* An' I'm gonna strangle whoever did this shit with my bare hands, you hear me? Bare hands!"

Danthres laughed.

"What's so funny, bitch?"

She shook her head. "You really expect me to believe that you're not jealous of them?"

"They was my best friends! We been through hell an' back t'gether, an' we *always* come out smellin' like roses, an' when I get my hands on that damned shit-sucking wizard, I'm gonna cave his head in!"

Finally, Torin thought. "What wizard?"

Bogg's expression suddenly changed to that of a small child who'd been caught with his hand in a jar of sweets. "Well, uh, stands t'reason, right? Gotta be a wizard doin' this. I mean, you guys'd've nailed the bastard by now otherwise, right?"

Torin leaned back in his chair. This was his favorite part of the interview process. All the bluster had flown from the barbarian's tone. His massive hands, which had been clenched into bludgeonlike fists, were now open, and his gestures, which had, consciously or not, been calculated to be as menacing as possible, now were more like flails.

"Actually," Danthres said, "the M.E. detected no magic whatsoever. So it can't possibly be a wizard."

"Which leads us to wonder who is responsible if not a member of the mage community," Torin said.

"Whaddaya mean no magic?" Bogg's eyes went wide at that. "That ain't possible. 'Sides, Genero said—" He cut himself off.

Leaning forward again, Torin said, "What did Genero say?"

"Nothin'," Bogg said in a quiet voice. "Never mind. Look, you got anythin' else t'ask me? 'Cause I'm gettin' tired'a this."

"That's too bad," Danthres said, "because we've only just begun. What wizard are you talking about?"

"I dunno—some wizard. Like I said, stands t'reason, right? Look, why you houndin' me for? I'm the guy whose friends're dead."

"Yes," Danthres said, "and you and your remaining friends have been withholding information from us—information that might have allowed us to find the killer and prevent more murders from occurring. Instead, we've been chasing our tails for days while you're treated to the luxury of this castle."

Now Bogg's bluster returned. "You say that like it's *good.* I hate this shithole. *Real* men don't sleep on silk with a stone roof overhead—gimme the great outdoors any night. It makes it easier to get to the fight."

"What fight?" Torin asked. "Whose head did you want to cave in, Bogg?"

Bogg stared at Torin, then stared at Danthres, then thought better of it and went back to staring at Torin. "Hell with it," he finally said, now staring down at the floor. "I'm sick'a this shit anyhow. Genero said it was the right thing to do, but he don't know everythin', and neither does that bitch-queen of a goddess of his." He looked back up at Torin. "Chalmraik."

"Chalmraik's dead," Danthres said. "Try again."

Bogg actually laughed at that. "Yeah, that's just what I said to Genero. But Temisa gave 'im one'a those visions'a hers. She don't give 'im visions all that often, but in all'a years I known Genero—an' we go *way* back—she ain't never given him a wrong one. Found *that* out the hard way."

As he said that, he absently rubbed one of the scars on his side. Torin wondered what the story behind that was, but didn't wish to get sidetracked, and so instead asked, "What did this vision entail?"

"That Chalmraik was still kickin', and was holed up on some island out on the Garamin. Genero gathered us all up at Velessa, then we came here t'get a boat."

Again, Torin leaned back. The other boot had *finally* dropped. He also remembered Danthres telling him earlier about Horran's story of the two self-styled heroes who literally fell all over themselves in the Docklands yesterday morning, trying to commission a ship to fight a revived Chalmraik on some island in the Garamin. *This is starting to pull together.* "Any particular resason why you all kept this from us?"

Bogg snorted. "Genero. He said you guys couldn't handle Chalmraik, an' that tellin' ya'd just putcha in danger."

"*Did* he, now?" Danthres said in a dull monotone, indicating that she was as aggravated as Torin himself felt. Neither of them particularly appreciated civilians presuming to tell them how to do their jobs—or not do them, as the case may be.

"So you gonna let us go beat his head in, or what?"

Torin stood up. "Or what, for the time being, I'm afraid. We need to go deal with some other matters. Wait here, please."

The fists came back. "I don't *wanna* wait here, I wanna—"

Danthres walked up to him. Though she was tall for a woman, he still towered over her. That didn't stop her from looking up at his ugly face and saying, "What you want is of no interest to us, barbarian.

Right now, I'm not convinced that you haven't been lying to us about Chalmraik and that *you're* the guilty one. Now you can either sit here or sit in the hole, it makes no difference to me."

Bogg stared down at her for several seconds. Then he turned and slammed his fist into the table a second time.

This time it broke the table in half.

As he exited the interrogation room, Torin said, "I'm afraid we're going to have to bill you for that."

Six

"Well, it's about damn time *somebody* arrived!"

Lieutenant Dru exchanged a glance with Lieutenant Hawk as they approached the apartment house. The woman standing in the doorway wore a battered housecoat, had a nose that was too big for the shape of her head, eyes that were too small for the rest of her face, hair that was too unkempt to be believed, and a voice that was too deep for her gender. Though she was obviously human, Dru had to wonder if she had some troll in her blood, especially given her girth, which almost exceeded that of the doorway.

"Excuse me?" he said.

"I sent that damn boy out two hours ago to fetch one'a ya! He's been goin' at it for longer than that, an' I'm *sick* of it!"

Again, Dru looked at his partner's dark face; this

time Hawk shrugged, his dreadlocks bouncing. They had come here because Jonas informed them of a sighting of their rapist suspect going into this building. They had been about to head home for the day, but—as this was their first actual lead and all—they decided to follow up on it. So they wended their way through the ever-darkening streets of Dragon Precinct, which were illuminated only by recently lit torches—Dragon couldn't afford the magicked lanterns they had on the streets of Unicorn. Several people recognized what their brown cloaks symbolized and asked if they were going to capture whoever murdered Gan Brightblade and/or Olthar loth-Sirhans.

"Hell," Hawk had said after the fourth time they had responded negatively, "we should just be sayin' yes. Beats seein' that look on they faces."

Dru had just shrugged and run his hands through his close-cropped brown hair. "No big deal."

"To you, maybe. Torin and Danthres, they be gettin' all'a good cases, all'a overtime—"

"—and all the shit from the other side of the castle. I'm all for the overtime, but I can live without meetings in Rom-Shit's office. Remember that crap with his nephew?"

Hawk had nodded gravely. Sir Rommett's nephew was the prime suspect in a double murder—of which he turned out to be innocent, but Rommett had spent so much time twisting himself into a pretzel to protect the boy from the charges that he made it damn near impossible for them to investigate. If the chamberlain had simply left well enough alone, they would have found the real killer in less than a day, and that would have been that.

"Course," Hawk had said, "we still got Osric on our asses 'bout this rapist."

"Osric's *always* on our asses. That's how we know he's awake. But I can't just laugh off the shit the way Torin does, and I *sure* as hell don't have the balls to mouth off at the uppers the way Danthres does." Dru had shuddered, remembering the reaming he'd gotten from Sir Rommett in his office. Scared to death of losing his job and its concomitant pension, which would allow him and his wife and kids to retire in peace in some nice city very far from Cliff's End, Dru just sat there and took it, nodding and saying "Yes, sir" a lot. It was the most humiliating experience of his life, and he had no urge to repeat it.

"Yeah, well, don't be praisin' Danthres's balls *too* much. She keep up like this, she gonna get the big boot, and then *we're* gonna get the shit. 'Cause you can guaran-damn-tee that they ain't gonna give Gan Brightblade's murder to Iaian an' the fish."

Eventually they arrived at the apartment house. The informant—a merchant who worked the corner diagonally across from the intersection where the house was located—assured Dru and Hawk that a man matching the description he'd been given by the guard who walked this beat went into the house and hadn't come out. The guard in question—an alert young man named Kellan—verified the merchant's story.

Now they stood in the doorway, confronted by this woman from hell. "Who are you, ma'am?" Dru asked before they went any further.

"I run this place—it's a *nice* place, an' that's 'cause I don't let this sorta thing go on."

"What sorta thing?" Hawk asked.

"Fornicatin'!" she practically screamed. "I won't have it, but that damn bastard's been at it for hours! An' I can't get the damn door open!"

"Don't you have a key?"

"Bastard changed the lock," she muttered. "That's against the lease agreement, by the way. He's a fornicator *and* a contract-breaker! I want him arrested!"

Dru shook his head and looked again at Hawk. The latter shrugged. If this woman ran the building, they'd need her cooperation to find the rapist. And dealing with this particular domestic squabble would probably get on her good side. *Assuming she has one. Hell, she probably hates fornicating so much because she doesn't get any practice.*

"Take us to the apartment, please, ma'am," Dru said.

They entered the lobby and started walking up the creaky wooden stairs. "You gonna break the door down?" she asked. "I can't afford to replace no doors. They're oak, y'know."

When they arrived at the top of the landing, Dru

saw that the doors, while wood, were *not* oak. The owner no doubt was hatching plans to overcharge when billing the city-state for replacing the door they were about to break. "No worries, ma'am. The door will be intact. We've got a skeleton key."

With that, Dru reached into a pouch in the belt he wore and pulled out a talisman in the shape of a skull. All the detective teams were issued these by the Brotherhood as a less destructive alternative to breaking down locked doors.

Troll-Woman led them to a door on the far end of the second story. Dru could hear the cause of her complaint from the moment they arrived on the landing. The moans, grunts, and groans of two people having very passionate sex echoed throughout the hallway, which made Dru wonder how loud it was *inside* the apartment. He also wistfully wondered why he and his wife never made that much noise anymore.

"See what I mean? Fornicatin'." Troll-Woman shook her head. "First Gan Brightblade, then Olthar lothSirhans, now this. City's goin' straight to the sewer in a hurry."

Hawk grinned, his white teeth a contrast to his dark skin. "Shall we be tryin' the simple approach 'fore we break an' enter?"

Dru indicated the door. "Be my guest."

"What's the name, ma'am?" Hawk asked.

"Torval, but I'm just gonna call him 'bastard' from now on."

Hawk chuckled as he pounded on the door with a fist. "Mr. Torval, open up! This is the Castle Guard!"

To Dru's annoyance, neither pounding nor verbal imploration had any discernible impact on the moaning, grunting, or groaning.

"Okay," Dru muttered and held the skull in proximity to the lock. He concentrated. The way Boneen explained it to him the one time he asked—well, actually, the twentieth time he asked, and the M.E. finally realized that he'd get no peace until he provided the lieutenant with an explanation—was that the skull housed a spell that would focus the wielder's concentration and open any nearby lock. It didn't seem to matter what one concentrated on—it was force of will that triggered the spell—so Dru thought very hard about how much he wished they could have the unlimited overtime Danthres and Torin had.

The eyes of the skull glowed even as the door made a satisfying clicking noise.

Then the door made another clicking noise. Frowning, Hawk tried it, only to find that it was again locked. "Shit."

Dru shook his head. "He must have the door magicked. How the hell does someone living in this shithole afford a Locked Door Spell?"

"Hey!" Troll-Woman said. "I run a good home here!"

Ignoring her, Hawk held up his arms. "I ain't gonna be bustin' down no more doors. Cap'n tol' me the next Healing Spell for my shoulders'll be comin' outta my damn paycheck. I got a family to support."

"You got a father who knows his son's a soft touch." Dru sighed.

"Hey, he's a cripple."

Dru started to say something, then thought better of it. Everyone knew that Hawk's father was no more crippled than Hawk himself. However, occasionally complaining about how much his leg hurt was enough to convince his son that he should support the old man with his Guard wages.

"Let me try again." He held up the skull and concentrated again, this time on how much he wished his partner would wise up and make his father get a damn job.

This time it took an extra second for the second click to relock the door.

"Shit. Guess we gotta break it down," Hawk said.

"No, wait," Dru said, putting a hand on Hawk's arm. "I think I'm making progress."

He held up the skull a third time and thought very long and very hard about how much he wanted his wife to make the noises he was hearing from the female half of the couple on the other side of the door.

The door clicked only once.

When in doubt, go for sexual frustration, Dru thought as he put the skull back in his belt. Hawk grinned and opened the door.

The apartment they saw was fairly nondescript. It was a one-room affair, with a waste bucket in one corner, a basin in the opposite corner, one filthy window in the center of one wall, another wall covered in shelves that were stuffed with various pieces of parchment, and no furniture save a very large bed.

On that bed were two humans. The woman seemed to be glowing slightly. She had no obvious reaction to Dru and Hawk's entrance.

The man—Torval, presumably—did, however. He looked up in shock.

That shock was matched by the two lieutenants, who found themselves staring at a man with small, beady eyes, a nose that had been broken more than once, oversized lips, thatches of hair on his cheeks that looked like a failed attempt to grow a beard, and enough hair all over the rest of his unclothed body for him to pass as an orangutan in a pinch.

This rather unfortunate concatenation of features matched that of the man Dru and Hawk last saw in Boneen's scrying pool when the M.E. showed them the results of the peel-back of the rapist's last victim.

"It's our guy!" Dru cried.

Torval leapt out of the bed and ran toward the wall with the window.

"Stop!" Hawk yelled. "Don't make—"

Then he ran *through* the wall—again, just as he had in the images Boneen had shown Dru and Hawk from each of the crime scenes.

True, they had known he was capable of this—it was why he'd been so damned hard to catch, as the guards who had chased him said—but it was still fairly disconcerting to see it up close like that.

As soon as he had left the bed, the woman disappeared in a puff of smoke, which, along with the glow, identified her as a sex-simulacrum.

Dru immediately turned and ran out of the apartment. He almost knocked Troll-Woman over on his way out, let out a hasty "Excuse me," and ran down the stairs, taking them three or four at a time. As he ran, he thought, *How the hell does someone who lives in this dump afford a Walk Through Walls Spell, a Locked Door Spell,* and *a sex-sim?*

Only when he reached the street did he realize that Hawk hadn't followed him. *Some partner,* he thought, irritated. Hawk could usually be relied upon to have Dru's back.

Putting Hawk's odd behavior aside, he turned his attention to the street. Unfortunately, not only was there no sign of a naked man running through the street, there was no sign that anyone had seen one. The latter wasn't necessarily conclusive, as it was dark and folks in this neighborhood tended to mind their own business, but still . . .

"Something wrong, Lieutenant?"

Dru turned to see Kellan jogging up to him. "Did you see him?"

"See who?"

"Dammit." Dru looked up at the side of the building. The other side of the wall that Torval ran through was open space, but it wasn't far above the roof of the building next door. Even barefoot, Torval probably easily ran off up there without anyone noticing, especially with the building cornices shadowing the rooftops from the street lanterns.

He turned back to Kellan. "Get the word out—we've got our rapist. His name is Torval, and right now he's running along the rooftops of Dragon, totally naked. *Find* him."

Kellan quickly nodded. "You got it, sir. We won't let him stop us now."

"If you see one of the youth squad—"

"Right 'ere, sir."

Dru turned around again, and looked down to see a young man dressed in rags that barely fit and dirt streaking his face.

"Hear tell you found'a rapist," the boy said. "He 'round?"

"Not yet, but we've got a name. Listen, I need you to run to Dragon Precinct and tell Sergeant Kel to put out a search for a naked man matching the description of the rapist—his name is Torval—and get the M.E. over here to check his apartment. You got that?"

"No problem, sir," the boy said in tones much more deferential than members of the youth squad usually employed. Dru reached into a pouch on his belt to fetch a copper piece, but the boy put up his hand. "This one's free. That Torval guy? He raped m'mom. Whatever you need, you got from me."

There were tears welling in the boy's eyes as he ran off. Now that Dru thought about it, he saw a resemblance between the kid and the second victim. *We'll get him,* Dru thought.

" 'Ey, Dru! Get your bony ass up 'ere!"

Dru looked up to see Hawk sticking his head out of Torval's apartment. "What're you still doing up there?" he asked angrily. "You're supposed to be my partner, an—"

"Shutcha damn mouth and start gettin' your damn ass up those damn stairs and back in this *damn apartment!*"

Blinking a few times, Dru stood his ground before finally commencing to move back into the building. *Wonder what he found up there.*

He ran back upstairs, his sword banging against his leg. When he reentered Torval's room, he asked, "All right, what's so important that—?"

"Look at these shelves."

Dru looked again at the shelves that lined one wall—as before, they were stuffed to the brim with assorted loose parchments. He turned back to Hawk. "It's full'a parchments. So what? You're my *partner*, you're supposed to—"

Hawk shoved one of the parchments into Dru's face. "Will you *look* at it?"

Angrily, Dru snatched the parchment from Hawk's hands. "I don't see what the big—"

Then he saw it.

The topmost portion of the parchment had the image of a male face with leaves and branches growing out of several orifices: the symbol of the Brotherhood of Wizards. The words on the page were in the stylized script that all spells were composed in.

Dru turned the parchment over—no sign of a seal, no wax residue. "Shit—this is the motherlode. Unsealed spells." He looked up. "Least now we know how he afforded all those spells. They were on his damn shelf."

"We gotta be gettin' Boneen down here right damn quick."

"Way ahead of you," Dru said. "I sent one of the kids to fetch him, and to get Dragon to put the eyes out on Torval."

Hawk was, at this point, grabbing parchments at random off the shelves. "Good. 'Cause we just be gettin' him on a lot more than jus' some rapin'. Look at this. Illuminate. Floor Sweep. Laundry. Flavor. Entrap Woman. Entrap Man. Entrap Troll." His face broke into a massive grin. "We gonna be the heroes'a Cliff's End by sunup for this."

Dru shook his head. "Like hell. This jackass was probably supplying half the city with bootlegged spells—and probably cheaper'n the Brotherhood was sellin' 'em. You think the people 'round here are gonna *thank* us for taking that supply away? Nah, all we did was make the Brotherhood's job easier—and you can for damn sure bet that they'll take all the credit for this. Or worse, brush it away, so no one knows that there ever was a bootleg spell seller. Shit, they'll probably raise their prices, too."

"You too damn cynical, Dru."

"Maybe."

Then Dru thought about the kid whose mother was raped. Now they had a name, a confirmed face, and a place of residence. Not only that, but with this new evidence, they'd probably have the full resources of the Brotherhood to track this guy down. That was why he expected the Brotherhood to downplay Dru and Hawk's own role in the whole thing.

But if it gets that kid's mother's rapist off the streets . . .

"Come on," Hawk said, "let's be goin' through these, see what kinda stuff our boy been up to."

Dru smiled. "Right with you, partner."

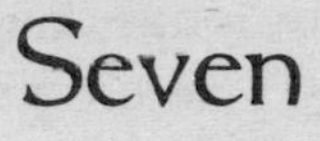

Seven

"Chalmraik the Foul was killed over a decade ago."

That was the first thing that Lord Ythran said when Danthres entered the mage's office, Torin by her side, before either even had the chance to sit down. The local official in charge of Brotherhood affairs for the region including Cliff's End, Ythran maintained this office in his mansion on the outskirts of the city-state. Despite Danthres carrying the Lord and Lady's seal (generously provided by an obsequious Sir Rommett and a frightened Bertram), she and Torin had been kept waiting almost two hours before Ythran deigned to see them this morning.

Talking to the Brotherhood was not a step Danthres was eager to take, but Osric insisted it had to be the next one, even before speaking to Genero and Ubàrlig (whom Jonas had sent away with apologies after Bogg's interrogation the previous night). After all, the Brotherhood *did* regulate magic in Flingaria—in fact, the organization was formed after the overthrow of Chalmraik specifically to avoid someone like him coming to power again. If the Foul One was still alive, they needed to know about it, Osric said. Somewhat reluctantly, Danthres agreed, as did Torin. And so, first thing in the morning—when Torin finally showed up to work—they proceeded through Unicorn to Ythran's mansion.

"Didn't Chalmraik come back from the dead once before?" Danthres asked as she took her seat on the sofa opposite the wizard's plush reclining chair. Ythran's office was an elegant affair, appointed with what Danthres assumed to be the finest furniture—including a small, overly decorated stone scrying pool—and several art objects. The east wall's centerpiece was a bas-relief of the Brotherhood's seal, and the rear wall was taken up entirely with a huge picture window providing a view of the Garamin.

"Not quite," Ythran said testily. He snapped his gnarled fingers, and a mug full of some kind of steaming liquid appeared in front of him. Grabbing it out of the air, he sipped from it. After wiping his robed sleeve over his bearded mouth, he let go of the mug, and it disappeared.

Damned showoff, Danthres thought. *And thank you for offering to share.*

The white-haired old man continued. "Chalmraik faked his own death via magical means. It was an impressive spell, in fact. However, that was *not* coming back from the dead. Now then, if you are through wasting my time—"

Danthres started to snarl, but Torin cut her off—which, she had to admit, was probably wise of him. "Lord Ythran, we have barely begun. Wc have very good reason to believe that Chalmraik might be alive and well, and targeting people in Cliff's End."

Impatiently, Ythran said, "I am fully aware of the complaint registered by Brother Genero of Velessa. I scried the report made by the Velessan office when you arrived at the mansion. I'm afraid that I have to give you the same answer they gave the priest. Besides, dead or alive, Chalmraik is *our* problem, not yours. So this is not your concern from any angle."

"If he's killing people in our city—" Danthres started, but Ythran interrupted.

"He isn't. Even if he somehow managed to resurrect himself—which he couldn't possibly have done without our knowledge, as that would require an expenditure of magic that could not possibly go unnoticed—he would not resort to such petty tasks as the murder of inconsequential non-mages."

Torin let out something that was halfway between a bark of laughter and a snort of derision. "I'd hardly call Gan Brightblade or Olthar lothSirhans inconsequential."

Ythran gave Torin a withering look. "It depends on what you consider to be of consequence. In terms of what actually matters in the universe, the antics of a buffoon who thinks with his sword and an overly romanticized traitor to his people are of very little moment. It is blindingly obvious that these people are lying to you."

Torin leaned forward. "You realize that you're accusing a Temisan priest and a respected dwarven general of fabricating a story."

Danthres refrained from pointing out that the Temisan priest in question had already lied. That was a nuance that was likely to go over the wizard's head—or, more accurately, be beneath his notice—in any event.

Letting out a long breath through his irritatingly perfect white teeth, Ythran said, "I'm not accusing anyone of anything, Lieutenant. Chalmraik the Foul cannot possibly be responsible for these murders. I'm sure it's quite possible that Brother Genero believes the vision he claims to have seen, and I'm equally sure that he believes that Chalmraik is responsible for these murders. However, in that at least, he is quite mistaken. This is an ordinary set of murders, and that falls under your purview, Lieutenants, not ours, so I'll thank you not to involve us in it."

It took most of Danthres's willpower not to laugh in Ythran's face. Usually it was she who pointed out that the Brotherhood was interfering in *her* affairs, not the other way around.

Torin, meanwhile, had no apparent interest in laughing. "There's nothing 'ordinary' about these murders, Lord Ythran."

"Perhaps not, but I believe that your own magical examiner determined that no sorcery was involved. Therefore it is not our concern. I'm afraid you will have to actually do your jobs rather than try to fob off responsibility on us, as your tiresome Guard has done so often in the past."

This time, Danthres's willpower was directed toward not strangling Ythran where he sat. Torin shot her a look, as if to make sure she did no such thing, but even she wasn't as foolhardy as that. Idiots like Sir Rommett were one thing, but, as tempting as it was, Danthres wasn't about to antagonize someone who could turn her into a farm animal without much effort.

"What was that?" Ythran asked suddenly.

Frowning, Torin said, "I didn't say anything."

"Neither did I," said Danthres.

The wizard waved his arms dismissively. "I'm not talking to you. Say that again." The second sentence appeared to be directed at the air to the left of Ythran's ear.

Danthres shook her head. *I hate magic.*

"Really? Oh dear. Oh dear oh dear oh dear. Yes, of course, I'll deal with it. Damn."

"Something wrong?" Danthres asked, trying to sound polite, and probably failing miserably.

"I'm afraid something"—now Ythran smiled, a

most unpleasant expression that had no business on his wizened face—"consequential has turned up. As much as I've enjoyed this total waste of time, I'm afraid that I have important matters to deal with. Ironically, it involves two of your fellows. They found some unregistered spells last night."

Danthres let out a breath. They had, of course, heard about Dru and Hawk's discovery at headquarters last night before going off shift. Torval, the rapist, was still at large, but at this point, it was only a matter of time before he was found.

"I need to deal with this immediately." Ythran stood up from his recliner.

Again, Ythran snapped his fingers—

—and Danthres found herself with a queasy feeling in her stomach and a sudden pounding headache. The contents of her stomach shot into her throat, and she felt her entire body clench. Before she knew it, she was doubled over, retching onto the stone floor.

Two heaves later, she stood up and realized that she was in Osric's office. Torin was standing behind her, a look of concern on his face.

Blinking tears from her eyes, Danthres said, "Bastard teleported us, didn't he?"

Torin nodded.

A familiar, angry voice from behind them bellowed: "What the hell is that smell?"

Danthres turned to see Osric standing in the open doorway. Danthres couldn't ever remember seeing quite that look of befuddlement on the captain's face before.

"Tresyllione, ban Wyvald, what the hell're you doing in my office?"

"Throwing up, Captain." Torin grinned. "I'm afraid the good Lord Ythran decided to cut our interview short by using a Teleport Spell on the pair of us."

Dryly, Osric said, "How generous of him."

"Have I mentioned how much I hate magic?" Danthres asked as she got to her feet. Her stomach still felt like a fist was clenching it.

"Once or twice." Torin was still grinning.

"What did he say?" Osric asked.

At that, Torin's grin faded. "Nothing useful."

"Oh, I wouldn't go that far," Danthres said. "He spent the entire time trying and failing to mislead us."

Osric held up a hand. "Hold that thought." He summoned Jonas to his office, told him to get someone to clean up the mess Danthres made, then adjourned to their desk. Danthres would have preferred sitting opposite Osric in his own domain instead of having him loom over them in their space, but needs must as the demons drive.

"All right," Osric said once they'd settled at Torin and Danthres's desk. Danthres had slipped into the pantry to get a mug of tea to settle her stomach, and now she sat in her chair, Torin in his spot opposite her. Osric stood over her with his arms folded, staring at her dolefully with his good eye. "What do you mean by 'failing to mislead us,' Tresyllione?"

"Wizards are rotten liars. Probably because words are so important to what they do, they can't afford to misuse them." She leaned back in her chair and took a sip of the tea. As usual, it was too bitter. "He was trying to convince us that Chalmraik was dead and not involved in this case, but he never actually came out and said that. As soon as we came in, he said that Chalmraik was killed over ten years ago. Not that he was dead now, but that he was killed. Later he said that if he was resurrected they'd know about it, and it would be their concern. But he never said that Chalmraik is dead now, nor that he hadn't actually managed to resurrect himself."

Torin scratched his beard. "It's rather clever, actually—it protects them from any accusations of having lied to us."

Osric shook his head. "I think you might be reading too much into this."

"No, we're not." Danthres leaned forward, putting the tea down on her desk. "Bogg only told us about Chalmraik because he let it slip by accident. He's not clever enough to have done that deliberately to throw us off a scent. Genero, Ubàrlig, and Bogg—"

"And presumably," Torin put in, "Brightblade, lothSirhans, and the halflings."

"—genuinely believe that Chalmraik is alive and a

viable threat. They also believe that he's the one targeting them. At this point, they have no reason to lie, and no real reason for us to believe they are lying."

Torin started fiddling with a paperweight on his desk. "The Brotherhood, on the other hand, has every reason to lie, especially if Chalmraik really is alive. Can you imagine what kind of outcry *that* would produce?"

Osric let out a breath. "Wonderful. So we have an all-powerful mass-murderer on our hands, and the organization best suited to deal with him won't admit he's alive. Where does that leave our case?"

"Nowhere at the moment," Torin said glumly.

Danthres found words pouring out of her mouth without conscious thought: "Why don't we go to that island?"

Osric and Torin both stared at her. "What?" the former asked.

Shaking her head, Danthres said, "No, never mind, it's a crazy idea." *What the hell were you thinking?* Grabbing the mug, she sipped more tea, figuring the upset stomach was addling her brain.

"Damn right it's a crazy idea," Osric muttered.

"Chalmraik's the most brutal tyrant Flingaria has ever seen," Torin said, his green eyes wide with incredulity. "What do you expect to do, waltz onto the island, tell him he's under arrest in the name of the Lord and Lady, and bring him into the interrogation room, hoping he'll crack?"

Danthres sighed. "I *said* it's a crazy idea, Torin, you can drop it now."

"Besides," came Boneen's irritating voice from behind her, "it's not like he's the murderer."

Turning, Danthres saw the M.E. waddle into the squad room on his undersized legs. Osric asked, "Don't you have to work on those spells?"

Boneen closed his eyes and let out a long breath. "Don't remind me. I swear, it's enough to drive a man to drink. First you two with your impossible case," he said with a sneer at Torin and Danthres, "and now I'm going to be drowning in unregistered spells for the next week thanks to those other two idiots. With my luck, Iaian and Grovis will find the fake-glamour ring and I'll have to do something connected to *that* as well."

Dryly, Danthres said, "It must be terrible, having to actually do your job."

"Don't get snooty with *me*, Tresyllione. I'm here as a favor to you lot, and it's a favor that you haven't earned, let me tell you."

Folding his arms, Osric asked, "Did you come in here for a reason, Boneen?"

"Hm?" The M.E. stared at the captain for a moment with his mouth hanging open. Danthres thought he looked like a fish—or like Grovis. "Oh, yes, I did. I'm on my way to help gather up those damned spells right now, but I wanted to let you know that I found something peculiar on one of the halflings. He owned a Charm Bracelet."

"Probably helped with the marks," Danthres muttered.

"You'd know more about that than I would." Boneen spoke with his usual disdain. "But I can't see why it didn't register on the peel-back. Admittedly, it's minor magic—just enough to make someone pay attention when you speak and be slightly more open to your words than they might be otherwise. I probably just missed it with everything else that's going on."

"No, that fits." Torin got up and started pacing. Danthres knew this meant he had an idea, so she let him talk. "I have a source that informed me that Brightblade had a glamour potion in his system when he died, which matches the eyewitness accounts."

Danthres refrained from voicing her opinion on that source, especially with the captain present. Besides, it *did* explain the cleaning woman's noticing discrepancies in Brightblade's appearance, and now with this new information about the halflings . . .

"That's not possible." Boneen, as usual, spoke with finality. "If he had drunk a glamour potion any time in the previous week, I'd've detected it."

"But you didn't."

"Your source is wrong."

"I don't think she is, and her information fits." Torin turned to Osric. "Captain, I want to have Dragon round up some of the Dog and Duck's patrons, have them look at the body, see if they think he looks older now than he did when he was alive. If he was, it'll corroborate my source."

Osric nodded.

Danthres, however, was more concerned with how Boneen started the conversation. "Why are you so sure Chalmraik isn't the murderer?"

"What?" Boneen asked.

"When you walked in, you said that Chalmraik wasn't the murderer. Why're you so sure?"

"Several reasons. The most obvious is that he's supposed to be dead." Boneen shrugged. "Still, I suppose he could overcome that, seeing as how he was supposed to be dead at least twice before."

"Twice?"

Boneen nodded. "Oh yes. There's the time everyone knows about, of course, but there was another time before that, when he did manage to resurrect himself. Only a few wizards are aware of it, though."

Danthres shook her head in annoyance. *Another omission to add to Ythran's ledger.*

"But that's the other reason why it can't be him," Boneen continued. "Chalmraik was—is—was—whatever—many things, but subtle has never been one of them. Nor is he wasteful. If he wanted this group dead, he'd have wiped them all out at once. Picking them off one by one doesn't match his particular idiom."

"Yes, but resurrecting himself would require a great deal of power, wouldn't it? Perhaps he drained his resources."

Boneen snorted. "So he's killing them one by one through a means that isn't detectable by a peel-back? Ridiculous. Besides, there's no kind of practical magic that can do that sort of thing. In order to kill these people magically, he'd have to leave some kind of trail."

Torin asked, "Couldn't he mask the trail?"

"In a way, but there'd be a ripple effect of some sort. You can't really *block* magic, you can just manipulate it. But the scale we're talking about here is something that can't be easily hidden, and would take enormous power—not just the murders, I'm talking about the initial resurrection. Frankly, it's a great deal more power than is worth committing to murdering a few people, even ones as well regarded as Brightblade and lothSirhans, and certainly more than is worth committing to two halflings. And each time he did—bring himself to life, then kill Brightblade, then kill lothSirhans, *then* kill the halflings—the risk of exposure would be even greater. It would be progressively harder to hide it. But there have been *no* disturbances, *no* leaks, *no* indications *of any kind* that this level of power's being used on any of the four murders, nor have there been any kind of disturbances, leaks, or indications that someone has pulled off a resurrection. Believe me, the last time, half the wizards in Flingaria knew *something* major had happened, and a quarter of those knew that Chalmraik had reconstituted himself." Boneen let out a long, wheezy breath, which didn't surprise Danthres, as this was the longest collection of consecutive words she'd ever heard him utter. "Blocking one I can see. Blocking two, even, especially given Chalmraik's power. But all five occurrences? It's possible, I suppose, but so *extremely* unlikely as to be as close to impossible as makes no never mind." Boneen shook his head. "Damn you both, you'll make me into a gibbering madman."

Grinning, Torin said, "'Make' you?"

Boneen ignored the gibe as he headed for the exit. "I need to go to the house of this rapist-cum-black-market-spell-seller. Sometimes I wish we just let anyone use magic like the old days. It may have been more chaotic, but I got a lot more naps."

After the M.E. departed, Osric looked at Danthres and Torin each in turn. "So, is this a dead end or not?"

"Not." Torin sat back down. "Two of the bodies had magic on them that Boneen didn't detect."

"Possibly three," Danthres said, a thought occurring. "Thanks to the timely arrival of Sir Rommett, nobody did a thorough investigation of lothSirhans's body. What if he was carrying something magical as well?"

"Worth a look." Torin looked at Osric. "We should go check the corpse."

Osric's lips twisted. "Normally, that'd be Boneen's job."

"Yes," Torin said, "but he'll be busy for most of the

day going through those spells Dru and Hawk found."

"He hates it when anyone enters his work area. He'll carry on like trash about it for weeks."

This was an irrelevant concern as far as Danthres was concerned. "He's *been* carrying on like trash ever since Brightblade's body fell. What's one more thing he's complaining about amid the litany?"

As Danthres watched, several emotions played across Osric's face. She could tell his desire to see this case closed as fast as possible in order to get the Lord and Lady off his back warred with a desire not to piss the M.E. off.

As expected, the former won. Boneen was perpetually pissed off anyhow.

"Do it," the captain said, unfolding his arms.

Danthres was out of her chair like a shot.

She and Torin exited through the west-wall doorway and headed to the narrow, winding staircase that led down to Boneen's lair. As they proceeded, their way lit only by a pair of hand torches they'd grabbed on the way down, several odors started to creep into Danthres's nose, even as the air grew considerably colder, making her grateful for the warmth of both her cloak and her torch.

The staircase fed into a doorway. No hallway, no other access, just a tiny landing enclosed by two walls on the right and left, the staircase behind them, and a huge, imposing wooden door with an ornate knocker in the same gryphon image as that on the crest of Danthres and Torin's armor and cloak.

As they approached, the gryphon spoke, using a squeaky voice that was even more annoying than either Ep's or Boneen's, which Danthres would not have believed possible. "What do you want?"

"We need to check something," Torin said blandly.

"Who are you?"

"Lieutenant Torin ban Wyvald and Lieutenant Danthres Tresyllione."

"What case?"

"The murders of Gan Brightblade, Olthar loth-Sirhans, Mari, and Nari."

This was followed by a lengthy pause. Danthres assumed that the spell was verifying that they were really who they said they were, and probably cross-referencing the case with Ep's files. Despite herself, she was impressed with the complexity of the spell. *Not that it matters. Boneen doesn't like us to come down to his sanctum sanctorum, and this fake gryphon will probably tell us to go hang until the old bastard comes back.*

To her surprise, she then heard the click of the door unlocking. The squeaky voice said, "The items relating to the case in question will be glowing. You may touch them. If you touch anything else, neither I nor my caster will be responsible for the consequences."

The gryphon then went back to being an unmoving door knocker. Letting out a breath, Torin pushed the large door inward, and they went inside.

Before Danthres could open her mouth, Torin said, "I know, I know, you *hate* magic."

Danthres smiled even as she wrinkled her nose. "Actually, I was going to ask what that smell was."

"Which one?"

"Well, I can make out peat moss, several spices, and goblin dung, but the rest is a blur."

Torin grinned. "I bow to your olfactory superiority. I just know that it smells wretched."

"That it does." Danthres put her torch out, as the windowless room was lit by an unseen source. Then she looked around to see a massive space filled with tables, some holding bodies—all of which had the blue tinge of a Preservation Spell—others laden with parchments and various odd-shaped items, plus one in the corner piled with jars labeled in a language Danthres didn't recognize and containing both liquids and various combinations of plant pieces.

Seven blue-tinged bodies were on tables, and four of them were glowing. The other three belonged to the triple murder Danthres and Torin had closed a week earlier, on which the magistrate was scheduled to make a decision fairly soon. There was no hurry as far as Danthres was concerned—they'd captured the bastard who did it, and he'd rot in the hole until it was time for him to be hanged. She and Torin had done their job in bringing the killer to justice and had moved on to the next case.

Torin went over to the elf's body. Danthres couldn't help but notice that, even in death, Olthar lothSirhans looked arrogant and pleased with himself. Elves spent most of their unnecessarily long lifetimes cultivating that look, and it was one inheritance from her father she would happily live without.

In fact, he looks just like that child-killer I disembowelled.

She still recalled the smell of the bodies of the mass grave of dead half-breed infants she'd come across on her journey from her birthplace of Sorlin to the city-state of Treemark, and for a moment the memory of that foul odor overpowered the stink of Boneen's lair. Yet, when she tracked down and killed the highborn elf responsible for the murder of the children whose only crime was to be, like Danthres, born of both human and elven blood, she recalled no smell at all. It was as if such earthly concerns as stench were beneath elves. Still, the sneer on the murderer's face just before she sliced him open from stem to stern was just like the look that was forever etched on Olthar lothSirhans's face now. . . .

"Well, look at this."

At Torin's words, Danthres forced herself back into the present. "Look at what?"

Torin was holding a pouch, one of several that was attached to Olthar's belt, with one hand. With the other, he had removed a vial from the pouch. It was labeled in Ra-Telvish and full of a blue liquid.

"Even I know what that says," Danthres said. "'Healing.' That's a potion."

"And Healing Potions are *not* minor magic, yet Boneen didn't mention it, either."

Danthres nodded. "Much as I hate to admit it, your whore was right. Whoever killed these people used magic, and was able to hide it."

"Along with any other magic. Which puts Chalmraik right back on top of our list of suspects."

Eight

"I'm tellin' ya, I don't know nothin' 'bout nothin'."

Iaian sighed. He'd been getting variations on this answer for the past several weeks from all the possible sources of the bad glamours. None of the usual suspects were being especially helpful. The victims all got theirs from intermediaries, most of whom they couldn't identify. The few that could be identified were just facilitators, half of whom didn't even know what the merchandise was.

That, Iaian thought, *is the problem with a good law-enforcement system—it forces the criminals to get smarter.* In the old days in Cliff's End, when Iaian was a boy, crime was more rampant, but it was also fleeting and mostly committed by idiots. As a teenager, his home had been robbed several times, but the thieves were often incompetent, either stealing nothing of value, or dropping it on the front lawn, or leaving it in pawnshops that were easy to trace back. Now, though, the thieves were organized, making sure that the stolen merchandise couldn't be traced, since if they didn't do that, they'd be caught by the detectives of the Guard.

"Well," Iaian said to the latest in a series of ignorant witnesses, "if you do hear anything, let one of the guards know."

"Fine, whatever. Hey, listen, whaddaya care 'bout this, anyhow? Shouldn't you be out findin' who killed Gan Brightblade and that elf?"

Iaian tried not to sigh. "Other detectives are handling that case, sir."

"What, you ain't all handlin' it? I mean, it's *Gan Brightblade,* f'r Wiate's sake, not some rat off'a street."

Smiling falsely, Iaian said, "We've got our best people on it, sir. Thanks again for your help."

"Yeah, fine." The man shook his head as he walked off.

I hate this job, Iaian thought as he wandered down Auburn Way in the opposite direction from his erstwhile witness. One of the minor thoroughfares in Dragon, Auburn was nonetheless full of exactly the kinds of small shops and tiny business concerns that fronted things like this bad-glamour ring. After twenty-three years in the Guard, nineteen of them as a detective, Iaian knew most of the shop owners by name, and was intimate with the details of many of their personal lives. *At this point, I'd probably have an easier time remembering Shiftless Alberto's favorite color than I would my wife's. If this damn job didn't pay so well . . .*

He was heading for Minar's Emporium, the over-impressive name of the underimpressive shop where Grovis had allegedly found a lead. Considering that Grovis couldn't find his ass with both hands, Iaian had his doubts. However, he let his partner indulge himself, in part because they weren't especially burdened with good leads, so they might as well chase a bad one, and in part because it meant he could get away from the twit for a little while.

Just two more years, Iaian thought. Then he'd have his twenty-five and a massive bonus that would be enough to set up his wife in a big house in Unicorn, and leave him alone in their modest Dragon apartment to spend all his evenings on Sandy Brook Way indulging himself. They'd no longer need to maintain the pretense of wanting to have anything to do with each other.

As he entered Minar's, he heard Grovis's annoying voice: "—on't provide me with the information I desire, my good man, I can assure you that it won't go well for you. No, it won't go well for you at all."

Grovis was leaning on the glass counter in the small space, attempting to look intimidating. Like most of Amilar Grovis's attempts to do anything relating to police work, it was an abject failure, as evidenced by Minar standing behind that counter with his bread-loaf-sized arms folded over his barrel chest and looking almost bored.

"Look, Lieutenant, I been tellin' ya, I don't know shit 'bout these bad glamours. Only magic I sell's registered with the Brotherhood. I ain't stupid enough to do any'a that black-market shit."

"You expect me to believe that everything in this store is properly licensed and with proper provenance?" Grovis obviously wanted to sound tough, but to Iaian's trained ear he sounded only whiny.

"I don't give a shit what you believe, Lieutenant. Check my merchandise if you want, it's all legitimate. I ain't scared'a you, but I for damn sure'm scared'a the Brotherhood. See you put me t'sleep 'cause ya bore me, but I piss them off, and they'll put me to sleep more permanent-like."

Grovis was about to say something else, but Iaian chose that moment to speak up. "Let it go, boy."

Whirling around, Grovis favored his partner with an angry look. "I'm sure this gentleman knows something."

Minar unfolded his arms and set his palms down on the counter. "Only thing I know's this, Lieutenant: I hope you catch the bastards, 'cause it's hurtin' my business. Folks like them jus' make it harder for guys like me t'make an honest livin' in the magic trade." The shopkeeper let out a snort. "Shit, the Brotherhood'll prob'ly use this as an excuse t'raise their damn prices again. I've had t'mark up s'damn high I'm losin' business. Course, it just means the black-market shitbrains can just lower their prices even more, and screw me outta *more* business."

"Thanks for your time," Iaian said quickly before Grovis could say something else stupid—which was pretty much anything that might possibly come out of his mouth. He grabbed his partner by the arm. "C'mon, let's go."

Grovis didn't shake Iaian's hand off until they reached the street. "What did you do *that* for? I was *this close* to make him crack under the pressure!"

Iaian couldn't help but laugh in the other detective's face. "Boy, the only pressure he was under was from busting a gut laughing at you."

"Why do you always do this? Every time I get near a suspect, you undermine me and make me look like an idiot."

Sighing, Iaian said, "No, nature does that, boy, I'm just trying to keep you from shining a torch on it."

"And you keep calling me 'boy.' "

"That's because you *are* a boy, boy. I been doin' this job for longer than you've been alive."

"Maybe, but that doesn't automatically make you superior to me. You just assume that because I'm the son of a banker, I can't possibly be a good guard."

"No, I assume you can't possibly be a good guard because we've been partnered for six months and I haven't seen any evidence to convince me otherwise."

Before Grovis could embarrass himself with further attempts to defend an honor he never had, a familiar figure approached, wearing leather armor with the Dragon crest of the local precinct.

Smiling, Iaian greeted the young man. "Simon! What the hell are *you* doing out in daylight?"

"Double shift. Last night was my night off, too, but then Grint hauls my ass in at sunup—like I need to be up at this hour, ain't like I'm gonna make the flowers grow."

Iaian laughed. Simon had never been one for the daylight hours, so he had always requested night duty, even when he didn't have to.

"Anyhow, he says they need extra bodies on account'a that big bust your boys made last night. So I get to do two shifts in a row." He shrugged. "Can't complain about the extra coin, now, can I?"

Primly, Grovis said, "Lieutenants Dru and Hawk are of higher rank than you, Guard, and you will speak of them with respect."

Simon looked at Grovis like he had an additional head and laughed. "Who's this then?" he asked Iaian.

"My partner, Amilar Grovis. Feel free to ignore him, it's what the rest of us do."

"Grovis?" Simon frowned. "What, like the bank?"

"Harcort Grovis is my father, yes." Iaian's partner was the youngest son of the owner of the Cliff's End Bank.

"I thought that whole family got arrested in that scandal a few years back."

Iaian hid a smile even as Grovis replied with great indignation, "That was the previous owners! My father purchased the bank following the conclusion of that unfortunate business. I can assure you, my father is above reproach."

"For one thing," Iaian said, "he's smart enough to keep his youngest kid out of the family business." Harcort had, in fact, petitioned Lord Albin to allow his son to join the Guard "to make a man of him." In Iaian's considered opinion, Amilar didn't have the equipment for such a manufacture. However, Lord Albin acceded to the request, and instructed Captain Osric to make the young idiot a lieutenant (a lower rank would not be worthy of the Grovis family name, after all). Osric teamed him with Iaian, presumably on the theory that the veteran could teach the new kid a thing or two.

Either that or he figured that, with only two years left before I hit my twenty-five, I wasn't gonna complain. In that, at least, the captain was right. That Iaian only had two years left before his pension was the only thing that kept the banker's son alive.

"Look," Simon said, "I heard you caught the glamour case. I may have somethin' for you."

That got Iaian's attention. "Oh?"

"See, last night I was down Sandy Brook Way, over at Amelie's."

Grovis frowned. "Amelie's? That's a house of ill repute, is it not?"

Again Simon laughed. " 'House of ill repute'?

This guy's *really* your partner? You're not shittin' me?"

"The shit's on me in this case," Iaian said. He hadn't been to Amelie's in years—mainly because since becoming a lieutenant, he could afford a better class of nighttime companion, one that was both more adventurous and more discreet. After all, he had to at least maintain the pretense with his wife. He couldn't afford that place at the end of the Way that Torin was so keen on, but there were some other good ones on that end. Amelie's, though, was strictly pay-fuck-and-leave. *I can get that at home, though the pay comes in a different form.* "So what happened at Amelie's?"

"I think," Grovis said, "we all know what happened at Amelie's. What I fail to understand is why the tawdry exploits of a guard and his concubine are of any interest to Lieutenant Iaian and myself."

"Who writes your dialogue, Lieutenant? I swear, I only thought people talked like that in plays." Simon shook his head. "Never mind. Anyhow, I usually go with Maria, but my luck, it's *her* night off, too. So I go with someone else, someone *gorgeous*—name'a Connilee. Lotsa energy, too, lemme tell you." Simon grinned widely at that.

Kids, Iaian thought with the amused distance of one who had long since lost interest in this kind of goofiness regarding sexual exploits. "So what happened?"

Simon's face fell. "Let's just say she stopped being so gorgeous—right in the middle of it all! Put me *right* off my game. Never shriveled up so fast in my life."

Putting a consoling hand on Simon's shoulder, Iaian said, "Well, you're young yet. Amelie's, huh?"

The guard nodded. "I ran the hell outta there, but when I came on this morning, and saw the bulletin about your case, I thought maybe it might have something to do with the bad glamours."

Iaian nodded. "Good call, Simon. We'll take it from here. But, uh, we may need you as a witness, in case Amelie gives us shit. You know how these owners are—they're not gonna want to admit to us that one of their clients wasn't wholly satisfied, and they're sure as hell not gonna want anyone to know they're even using glamours, much less bad ones."

Simon shook his head. "Yeah, that's a *real* big secret. Hey, thanks, Lieutenant. Anything you need me to do, you let me know."

As the guard walked off, Iaian shook his head and smiled. The bulletin that was up on Dragon's board probably made mention of the priority the Brotherhood placed on this case. Simon no doubt figured that helping out on a case like this could only help his career.

"We're not really going down to that den of iniquity, are we?"

Iaian rolled his eyes. *I never used to roll my eyes.*

It's only since I was partnered with this infant. "What's your problem, boy?"

"Such activities as go on in places like that are an affront to Ghandurha."

"Yeah, well, this bad-glamour ring is an affront to the captain, the Lord and Lady, and the Brotherhood. Frankly, I'm more worried about them than Ghandurha, especially if we don't put this case down soon." Even as Grovis nervously made his religion's wards against evil with his hands, Iaian started walking down Auburn Way toward Meerka, which would take them to Sandy Brook. "Half the rich shitbrains in this town say they worship Ghandurha, but I swear, you're the only one who takes it seriously. You'd be better off with Wiate. He expects people to be hypocrites."

Grovis had nothing to say to that; he simply walked alongside Iaian.

When they reached Meerka Way and turned right, the young idiot said, "I don't understand what difference this all makes anyhow. As if it matters that some vain fools are taken by criminals. Serves them right for not knowing better. We should be solving *important* cases."

"Like the Brightblade murder?"

"Exactly!" Grovis practically skipped down the street, so excited was he by the prospect of handling that case. "That's what's important!"

"It's all important, boy. And none of it is."

Grovis frowned. "That doesn't make any sense."

"And *that* is why you're not a good guard." Iaian grinned. "When what I just said makes sense, then, maybe, you'll be a good one."

"You're just saying that to annoy me."

"Well, I have to get some of my own back," Iaian muttered.

As they proceeded down Meerka, several people inquired if they were going after the killer of Gan Brightblade and Olthar lothSirhans, which only served to worsen Grovis's mood. That, in turn, improved Iaian's.

By the time they reached Amelie's on Sandy Brook, Grovis seemed ready to jump out of his own skin. As they walked through the poorly carved wooden door, the boy had his hand on the hilt of his sword.

"You're not gonna need that," Iaian said with a sigh. "Or you think the average whore has combat training?"

Sheepishly, Grovis removed his hand from the hilt.

"Well, well, well," said a voice from behind the small desk in the back of the lobby area, which was otherwise appointed with several semi-comfortable-looking cushions. The room was empty aside from her and the two lieutenants, but it *was* still morning. . . .

"Amelie." Iaian nodded. "Long time, no see."

"And whose fault is that?" Amelie asked in a purring voice. She rose from behind the desk. The owner of the establishment wore a scoop-necked, skintight blue dress that accentuated a figure that showed no evidence of age. Her large breasts were as firm, her hips as supple as they were when Iaian first saw her twenty years ago. Iaian suspected the work of glamours that functioned better than the ones her employees used. "We never see you around here anymore."

"Sorry, not as partial to open sores as I used to be."

"You frequented places like this?" Grovis asked, aghast. "But you're a married man! That's adultery!"

"It's only adultery if you're sleeping with someone in addition to your wife," Iaian said, "which would require my sleeping with my wife in the first place." He turned back to Amelie. "I need to talk to one of your employees—Connilee."

"Connilee's not available."

Iaian smiled. "Right, 'cause her glamour went bad on her."

Amelie put her hand to her heart, which necessitated her resting her hand on her ample chest. Grovis, Iaian noticed, was staring openly, and Iaian wondered if Ghanduhar would approve of what the boy was thinking just then. "None of my women use glamours, Lieutenant, and I am offended that you would think they did."

"Cut the shit, Amelie. I've got a witness who says that Connilee was wearing a glamour that went bad on her right in the middle of sex."

Now Amelie put her hands on her hips. "Obviously your witness is lying."

Grovis found his tongue. "The witness in question is a member of the Cliff's End Castle Guard, and is therefore above reproach—even if he was frequenting such a foul place as this."

Amelie turned her gaze on Grovis. "Who are you?"

"This is my partner," Iaian said, "Lieutenant Grovis."

"Well, Lieutenant Grovis, I'll have you know that my place is quite clean and completely legal."

"One can be legal without being moral."

"Or one can be neither," Iaian put in, "especially if you're buying cheap glamours after the Brotherhood raised their prices again."

"That's crazy. I said we don't use—"

"Amelie, I can probably get the Brotherhood to give me receipts proving that they did sell glamours to you for the women. And then I can get them to investigate why they haven't sold as many recently. Then they might find out that you're using black-market glamours, and then they might get pissed. Or, should I say, more pissed. You heard about that bust last night?"

Amelie nodded.

"This bad-glamour ring has them livid as it is, and last night just made it worse. Trust me, you do *not* want to be in their scrying-pool range right now. So I suggest you produce Connilee so we can question her, find out where she got the glamour, and bust these guys, which'll make everyone happy."

Shaking her head, Amelie said, "You're still a bastard, you know that, Iaian?"

Iaian grinned. "Women keep saying that to me."

"Men, too," Grovis muttered.

"Connilee's really not here." Amelie pursed her lips. "After what happened last night with your guard friend, I sent her away. Believe me, if I'd *known* he was a guard—"

"Where'd you send her, Amelie?" Iaian asked.

"I'd rather not say where. She got the glamour from me, and I got it from a man named Antonio Markov."

Grovis asked, "And where can we find this Markov?"

"The docks, mostly. He has arrangements with a lot of ships."

Iaian snorted. "I'll bet. How'd you meet him?"

At that, Amelie smiled. "Same way I meet most men." The smile fell. "You'll probably find him on the north end of the Docklands, a small tavern called the Dancing Seagull. He always sits in the corner drinking coffee."

"Who goes to a tavern for coffee?"

Amelie shrugged. "He does, apparently. I've never seen him drink alcohol."

"Weird." Iaian shook his head. "All right, Amelie, thanks. And just for that, I *won't* tell the Brotherhood where I got my tip on where to find this guy."

"Really?" Amelie blinked several times, and then the purr returned to her voice. "You mean that, Iaian?"

"Yeah. I figure you're gonna have enough trouble, since you're gonna need to go back to paying the Brotherhood full price for glamours that actually *work.*"

She laughed. "Probably, yes. But still, I guess you're not a complete bastard after all." She walked forward and stroked his cheek. Her hand felt nice and smooth. Too smooth, truth be told. *Hell, she's probably not just wearing a glamour, she's probably got a potion.*

Then Amelie turned to Grovis. "You aren't related to Branik Grovis, are you?"

"He's my brother." Grovis frowned. "Why?"

"Tell him that he still owes me three silver for that statuette he broke last week. He won't get to sleep with Maria again until he pays up."

The look on Grovis's face at this particular revelation was, to Iaian's mind, worth the entire trip.

The same could not be said for the trip to the Dancing Seagull, which, to Iaian's chagrin, meant going to the Docklands. Iaian hated the entirety of Mermaid Precinct with a fiery passion, mainly because the sight, smell, and taste of fish made him sick to his stomach.

As he and Grovis crossed into Mermaid, the time-chimes rang twelve, and the fish smell was *everywhere*. The boats were all coming in with the morning catch and transferring their piscine cargo to the market for the afternoon shoppers to buy for the evening meal. The routine was the lifeblood of daily life on the docks, and midday was the smelliest part of it. Everywhere they turned, there were wheelbarrows full of fish passing, or crates of fish being carried, or bags of fish being exchanged. It was an orgy of seawater and scales, and Iaian thought he was going to throw up right there on the planks.

"Are you *quite* all right?" Grovis asked. "You look rather—green."

"I'm fine. Just don't like fish."

Grovis goggled at him, giving him an expression remarkably similar to that of the animal in question. "Don't like fish? How can you not like fish?"

"I just don't, all right?"

"For Ghandurha's sake, Iaian, you live in a port town."

Iaian gritted his teeth. On those rare occasions when she spoke to him, his wife often asked him why he chose to remain in a port town if he hated fish so much. *It just figures that this jackass would be parroting her.* Aloud, he said, "I was born in Cliff's End."

"So? Danthres was born in Sorlin, Osric was born in Iaron, and Torin was born in Myverin. They were able to move elsewhere."

"Because the one thing I hate more than fish is traveling."

"That strikes me as a very limited attitude," Grovis said with a sniff.

"Keep it up, and that's not the only thing that's gonna strike you." He peered up the docks, and saw a ramshackle wooden structure at the far northern end, on which perched several dozen seagulls, including three on the wooden sign that hung from a rusty metal rod that jutted from over the door. The words DANCING SEAGULL on the sign were mostly legible, obscured somewhat by splotches of seagull dung. Iaian wasn't sure whose sense of humor this said more about, the tavern owner's or the seagulls'.

The pair went inside, and it took Iaian's eyes a moment to adjust. The midday sun reflecting off the water made it unusually bright outside. Iaian hadn't really noticed until they went into the near darkness of the interior of the Dancing Seagull.

Like most taverns in Mermaid, the place was all but empty during the day. One customer sat at the far end of the bar; Iaian could smell the whiskey the man had been consuming from the doorway. A couple of dwarven sailors sat at the other end of the bar, their small legs dangling from the bar stools, engaged in conversation in their tongue, which Iaian had never mastered. A man stood behind the bar, cleaning glasses.

Sitting in a corner booth, a human was reading a piece of parchment, and sipping from a large mug of coffee.

"There's our man," Grovis said, indicating the corner booth.

"I was wondering what that wood-burning smell was," Iaian said as they walked to the corner.

"I beg your pardon?"

Iaian grinned. "It was you making an actual deductive process." Before Grovis could say anything, they arrived at the booth. The occupant took no notice of them, continuing to sip his coffee and read his parchment—which, Iaian noticed, was written in Ra-Telvish. *Pretty impressive—not many dock rats can even read Common, much less any other language.* "You Antonio Markov?"

"Depends."

Iaian frowned. "On?"

Markov took a long sip of his coffee. "Who's askin'?"

"I'm Lieutenant Iaian, this is my partner, Lieutenant Grovis."

"You're Guard."

"And your powers of observation are stunning. We have some questions for you about some merchandise you sold to—"

"Don't sell merchandise." Markov had yet to look up from his parchment.

Grovis stepped in. "We have it on excellent authority that you sold substandard glamours to one of the houses of ill repute on Sandy Brook Way. Now you will inform us—"

Now he looked up. "Talk to Gaffni."

Iaian frowned. Gaffni was the name of the new day-shift sergeant in Mermaid. He got the job after Sergeant Rai Victro was busted for several dozen counts of graft. This being Mermaid, Iaian's opinion was that the biggest crime Victro committed was being sloppy enough to get caught. "What about him?"

"He'll tell you. Don't sell merchandise. Gaffni knows all about me."

And Gaffni's picking right up where Victro left off.

Grovis stepped forward and leaned over Markov in a manner the young jackass probably thought was intimidating. "We're not talking to Gaffni, my good man, we're talking to you."

"Talk to Gaffni." Markov's voice was now getting insistent.

" 'Fraid it doesn't work like that, Mr. Markov," Iaian said. He sat down across from the man. "See, we're not with Mermaid Precinct. We work back at the castle. We report straight to Captain Osric."

Markov took another sip of coffee. "I don't know him. Know Gaffni. Gaffni told me, any problem with any of you Guard, I send 'em to him. So I'm sending you to him."

Iaian repeated, "It doesn't work like that. We're detectives. We've got a major crime ring, and we think you're supplying it."

"Don't supply nothin'. Talk to Gaffni."

Grovis slammed a hand down on the wooden table hard enough to make the dwarven sailors and the drunk at the bar jump. "I believe we informed you that we won't be speaking to Sergeant Gaffni, as we have no need. Now you will tell us what we wish to know, or I can assure you, my good man, that the consequences will be dire—most dire indeed."

"Talk to Gaffni."

Iaian was starting to get a headache, though how much of it was from Markov's repetition and how much from Grovis's stupidity he wouldn't venture to guess. "Mr. Markov, we need you to come with us."

"Ain't goin' nowhere. Talk to Gaffni."

"Is there a problem herc?"

Iaian turned around to see that a burly guard had entered the tavern. He barely fit in his leather armor, which was emblazoned with the crest of Mermaid Precinct.

"No problem, Guard," Grovis said. "We are simply questioning a witness in a very important case. There's no need for you to concern yourself."

Grovis turned his back on the guard, who had now reached the corner booth and was looming over the young lieutenant. *Oh shit,* Iaian thought as the guard grabbed Grovis by the shoulder and violently turned him around.

"If you're talkin' to Antonio, then I'm concerned, shitbrain. Whatever you got, ain't got nothin' to do with him, all right?"

"See here, Guard, I am Lieutenant Amilar Grovis. My partner and I are working on a case of critical import, and you—"

"I don't give a troll's ass what you're workin' on, Antonio ain't got nothin' to do with it."

"We have a witness who disagrees with you. Now kindly be on your way before we—*whoulff!*"

Iaian rolled his eyes. The guard had punched Grovis in the stomach. *I guess I'm going to have to defend him,* Iaian thought as his partner doubled over onto the filthy floor of the Dancing Seagull.

Standing, Iaian noticed that the two dwarves had departed the premises and the bartender was now on the far end of the bar from Markov's booth. The drunk hadn't moved, probably oblivious of all save the contents of his whiskey glass.

"You wanna piece'a this, too, old man?" The guard made a fist out of one meaty hand.

"Look, kid, I think you'd better lay off."

"I ain't no 'kid.' M'name's Paol Victro. Nobody harasses Antonio here without goin' through me."

I don't believe it, Iaian thought. He knew that Victro had several sons, but had no idea that any of them were guards. He shrugged and started toward the door. "All right, fine. We'll be on our way, then. C'mon, Grovis, let's go get the folks from the Brotherhood in, let them deal with it."

"Waitasec, what brotherhood?"

Holding back a smile, Iaian stopped in his tracks and turned around. "What Brotherhood do you think?"

"What, the damn magicians?"

"That would be them, yeah. See, Mr. Markov

here's our best lead on a bunch of bad glamours that've been showing up all over Dragon Precinct. The Brotherhood's *real* interested in who's muscling in on their territory. But hey, if you're willing to speak for Mr. Markov here, we'll just send the Brotherhood over to you."

But Paol Victro was no longer even paying attention to Iaian, having instead decided to loom over Markov who, for his part, continued to calmly sip his coffee and read his Ra-Telvish parchment.

"You stupid son of a goblin. Those glamours were *bad?* Are you out of your *mind?*"

Markov shrugged. "I just pass on the stuff from Cap'n Max."

"Dammit, I told you not to deal with Max no more!"

"He said he had good stuff."

Paol opened his mouth, but Iaian overlaid him. "Much as I hate to break up this lovers' quarrel, I'm gonna need *both* of you to come back to the castle with us. Sounds like we've got a whole lot to talk about."

"How many times?" Paol was shaking his head and still staring at Markov. "How many goddamn times did I tell you not to deal with that piece of shit? Max's stuff is *always* bad. *Always!* And you took *glamours* from him? What, did you *want* us to get caught?"

Iaian decided to throw caution to the wind and grab the larger man by the arm. "You coming along?"

Looking at Iaian's hand like it was a diseased rat, Paol started to tense, then visibly deflated. "What's the point? Brotherhood'll probably change me into a rat-creature or somethin' if I resist now."

"Wouldn't be much of a change, if you ask me. C'mon." Iaian led the guard toward the door. "Hey, Grovis," he called back to his still-doubled-over partner, "when you can breathe again, bring Markov with you."

"I want—I want—" Grovis got out between wheezes, "I want that man—arrested."

"Already doin' that, boy. Just bring the other guy."

Two more years, Iaian thought as he led out Paol, who was still muttering about Markov's stupidity to himself.

Nine

Torin glanced around at the interrogation room. The lantern was full of kerosene and casting sufficiently ominous shadows in the corners of the room. Toward the back of the room sat a small wooden table that had dozens of initials, figures, and other odd characters carved into it. Two steady wooden chairs had been placed on one side of the table. Against the back wall, facing the door and the two comfortable seats, was one rickety chair with uneven legs and a back that was angled in such a way as to make one's spine hurt after an hour or so. So many times Torin and Danthres had brought the dregs of Cliff's End into this room, sat them on that chair, and pried confessions out of them.

Somehow he doubted that such would be the case here. But it was long past time that they got a straight answer out of Brother Genero, and they were not going to let him out of the room until they got it.

Danthres led the priest in a moment later. Torin noted that his robes had been laundered since Danthres interviewed him at the Dog and Duck, giving him a fresher look in general. However, Torin also noted that the freshness didn't extend to his face—the priest had a haunted expression, and a look of genuine fear behind his eyes.

"Thank you for coming to see us, Brother," Torin said with his most pleasant smile. "I apologize for our inability to see you last night, but things have been a bit hectic here. You understand, of course."

Genero did not sound placated. "I'm afraid I don't understand, Lieutenant. You kept General Ubàrlig and me in those other rooms for *hours*. When the sergeant came to get us, we were told you'd gone home, and that we were not permitted to speak to each other. We were each brought to our rooms under guard. I don't appreciate this treatment, Lieutenants."

Indicating the uncomfortable chair, Torin said, "Have a seat, please, Brother."

"Why were we kept under guard and not allowed access to each other?" Genero moved toward the table as he asked the question.

"For your own protection," Torin said. "It was unavoidable, I'm afraid. You see, we had a break in the case that necessitated speaking to the Brotherhood of Wizards."

Genero halted in his tracks just before he reached the other side of the table. "I beg your pardon?"

"The Brotherhood. Unfortunately, we couldn't get an appointment to see their representative until this morning. A tiresome business, I can assure you—you know what bureaucracies are like."

Genero now took the seat. "I've had very few dealings with the Brotherhood. They tend to frown on priests, especially those who use magic."

"Yes, I've heard that." Torin took the seat opposite him. Danthres, who had remained quiet, stood behind Torin, arms folded over her chest. "In any case, I'm sure you know how difficult structures like the Brotherhood—or like the priesthood—can be."

"They can be, I suppose," Genero said slowly. "I have, I confess, played very little role in the mainstream of the Temisan priesthood."

Danthres finally spoke. "*That's* hardly surprising. You gallivant around in armor, carry a sword—it's a wonder they let you stay on at all."

Now Genero grew defensive. "Every action I have ever taken has been with the full blessing of the bishopric. They have approved of my actions over the years, and support my—" He hesitated.

"Adventures?" Danthres prompted.

"For lack of a better word, yes," Genero said weakly.

"Nasty business, adventures." Torin leaned back and smiled. "I've had plenty in my day, and I have to say that they don't track very well with spirituality."

Genero had folded his hands on the top of the table, and was now smiling serenely. "Then you've obviously had the wrong kinds of adventures, Lieutenant."

Laughing, Torin said, "Quite possibly, yes."

"What did we need to be protected from?"

Feigning ignorance, Torin asked, "What?"

"You said that Bogg and Ubàrlig and I were kept separate for our own protection. I have to confess that I find the entire concept ludicrous. Collectively, the three of us have faced threats that would drive most people mad, or kill them—or both. I very much doubt there is any protection we could possibly require from you. So my question to you, Lieutenant, is from what are you protecting us?"

Danthres said, "It isn't necessary for us to tell you that, Brother. You see, we're the Castle Guard. According to the Lord and Lady's edict, that gives us broad discretionary powers over those who walk within the boundaries of the demesne when we're in the midst of an investigation." She unfolded her arms and bent over, placing her hands on the table. "Which, in practical terms, means we can do whatever the hell we want."

Before Genero could respond to that, Torin spoke up. "As it happens, however, we *can* tell you in this case. You see, our latest information indicates that you're each in grave danger—and *not* from an old devotee of the Elf Queen."

"From whom, a wizard?" Genero asked, now taking the seat.

"Good guess," Danthres said snidely.

Now Genero turned his serene smile upon Danthres. Torin observed, however, that the fear behind his eyes was still there. "It was a logical deduction," the priest said, "given that you had to speak to the Brotherhood. However, I can't imagine who it might be. I've met many wizards in my time, as have the rest of us, but the only ones we ever ran afoul of are quite dead."

"Are you sure of that?" Danthres asked.

"Of course I'm sure. Ask anyone, they'll tell you that Chalmraik the Foul, Mitos, and Hwang are all dead. I've stood over the corpses of all three, and dedicated their souls to Temisa's mercies—though I doubt She was all that merciful with any of them, especially Chalmraik."

Torin regarded Genero with a serious expression. "I've heard that, if a wizard was powerful enough, he could resurrect himself."

"And where did you hear that?" Genero asked with a certain disdain.

"Oh, here and there. Do you believe that to be the case?"

"I do know that Chalmraik faked his own death years ago, but beyond that . . ." He shrugged.

"Interesting. So you don't believe that wizards can resurrect themselves?"

"I have to confess, I've never given it much thought."

Danthres started to pace across the room. "It's funny that you say what you said."

Genero smiled. "That I've never given it much thought?"

"No, before—that if you 'ask anyone,' they'll tell you that Chalmraik's dead. The same morning that we found your friend Brightblade's body, two men got into a fight on the docks."

"I daresay that sort of thing happens fairly regularly."

Danthres actually almost smiled at that. "Well, not that often in daylight. Do you know what these two men were fighting over?"

"A woman, presumably, or money," Genero said with a level of cynicism worthy of a member of the Guard. "I have found over the years that those are the most common reasons for men to brawl."

"Another good guess, but no." She stopped pacing and turned to face the priest once more. "They had both booked passage on the same boat, each with the stated goal of killing Chalmraik the Foul, who had resurrected himself and was plotting to try to take over the world again. But each of these men, armed with a sword blessed with the Runes of Tyrac—"

"The runes of what?" Genero asked, sounding genuinely confused.

"Tyrac," Torin repeated helpfully. "It's an old scam

that is generally pulled on strong, stupid types who want to live lives emulating that of—well, of you," he said with a smile, "and your friends. Both these men were convinced that they were destined to stop Chalmraik. For that matter, a teenager was arrested yesterday for opening a magical portal in his backyard. When they brought him in, he said he was studying magic clandestinely in order to protect his family from Chalmraik now that he was back from the dead."

"These rumors don't just start of their own accord," Danthres said. "All these people thinking Chalmraik is alive, and we have to wonder if maybe they're not onto something."

"I doubt they are." Genero now looked down at the floor.

"Now why do you say that?" Danthres asked. "You just said that you've faced three wizards and lived to tell the tale. That's no small accomplishment. You know how powerful they are, what they're capable of. Do you *really* think that they can't bring themselves back from the dead?"

"As I said, I haven't given it any thought." The priest spoke in a tight voice. "What is the point of this questioning?"

"I believe I told you," Danthres said, "that we're under no obligation to explain ourselves to you when you're part of our investigation."

"That may be true, but I also know that the three of us are guests of the Lord and Lady. I suspect that if I complain to them, they might take issue with the way you have been treating us. Honestly, Lieutenant, I don't see a vague, unconfirmed threat from a dead wizard is a good enough reason to keep the three of us from even speaking to each other."

Danthres barked a laugh. "That's where you and I differ, Brother—I don't see four murders as vague or unconfirmed."

"You know what I mean," the priest said dismissively.

"No, truly, I don't. And I don't see why you feel the need to hide behind the Lord and Lady now."

"I am not hiding—I've never hidden from a single thing in my life." He smiled, and Torin thought it a rueful one. "If I did, I never would have taken my oath to Temisa in the first place."

Danthres looked at Torin. "*I* think he's hiding behind the Lord and Lady, do you think he's hiding behind them, Torin?"

"Most definitely." Torin nodded his agreement.

"Now what reason would you have to do that, I wonder?" Danthres asked.

Genero stood up quickly, anger now making his face and mostly bald head start to turn a shade of red similar to that of his robes. "Possibly because you are abusing your authority as members of the Castle Guard! We have been *nothing* but cooperative with you since Gan's death, and you have rewarded us—"

"Sit down, Brother Genero," Danthres said in a low voice.

"I refuse to—"

Danthres moved around to the other side of the table and stood face-to-face with the priest. Since Genero was half a head shorter than Danthres, that meant she looked down on him with one of her fiercer expressions. "Sit. Down."

For a moment, Torin wondered if Genero was going to challenge her. If he did, he would be the first person in this room to do so.

Then, after they stared at each other for several seconds—during which Genero's color faded back to normal—he sat back down.

However, Danthres continued to stand in the same spot, now looming over him. "Frankly, Brother, I don't give a damn whether or not you tell the Lord and Lady that you've been mistreated, because it doesn't matter to me. What *does* matter to me is that four people are dead." She started to walk back toward the door. "If you want to go out and tell them that we've been mean to you, then you go right ahead. Maybe it'll cause problems for me down the line, but I don't give a shit, because *four people are dead*. That may not mean anything to you—"

Now Genero slammed his hand down on the table, his face turning the red color again. "It means *everything* to me! They were my dearest friends—and, as you insist on reminding me, four of them are *dead*. What's more, they were here at *my* instigation—in a way, I'm responsible for this, and I will not stand for—"

"Our finding the killer?" Torin said gently. "Our doing our jobs?"

That brought the priest up short.

Danthres stepped in, then. "You see, Brother, that's all that matters to me. The Lord and Lady may scream and wail, Captain Osric may give me a hard time, I may get called into some aristocrat's office and have my head handed to me, and I don't give a damn about *any* of it, because ultimately the important thing is that four people are dead, and I have the task of bringing their killer to justice." She pulled her earth-colored cloak halfway around her person. "This is my badge of office, and it means that I have been given a responsibility that's as important to me as I presume your responsibility to Temisa is to you—and as important as you *claim* your friendship with Brightblade and the others is. Torin and I"—and now she cast a glance over at Torin—"we speak for those who cannot speak for themselves. And we do not take kindly to those who obstruct us in our pursuit of that."

Genero shook his head. "That is a very pretty speech, Lieutenant, but wholly irrelevant."

Danthres barked a nasty laugh. "Really?"

"I have done nothing to obstruct your investigation, and neither have any of my comrades."

"On the contrary," Torin said, "you've done nothing but. When Lieutenant Tresyllione interviewed you, you expressed surprise that Mr. Brightblade might have been murdered. When we interviewed General Ubàrlig, he pointed us in the direction of an old follower of the Elf Queen."

"How is that unhelpful?" Genero asked, sounding incredulous.

"It's a lie." Danthres sat down on the desk, leaning over Genero in such a way that getting up would be awkward for him. "You *are* responsible for the deaths, aren't you, Genero?"

"Only insofar as I suggested this trip."

"You didn't 'suggest' anything," Danthres said. "You gathered them all up in order to fight one last foe. You brought them together in order to face Chalmraik, and Chalmraik killed them."

"That's ridiculous!" But even as he spoke, Torin saw the fear move to the front of his eyes. "You're actually putting stock in rumors about wizards' ability to resurrect themselves and the gossip of madmen on quests?"

"No." Torin stood up. "We're putting stock in our magical examiner, who told us in detail how Chalmraik came back from the dead once before, and in the testimony of one of your party."

Genero blinked. "What?"

Danthres smiled sweetly. "Bogg told us all about your quest last night."

"*That* was why we had to involve the Brotherhood."

Leaning back in his chair, Genero muttered something in a language Torin did not recognize, but suspected was an ancient Velessan dialect—he did catch the word *Temisa* as part of it.

"Would you care to explain why you left that rather vital piece of information out of your answers to Lieutenant Tresyllione's questions after Mr. Brightblade died?" Torin asked formally.

"It was for—" Genero cut himself off.

Then he laughed.

Icily, Danthres asked, "Would you mind sharing the joke, Brother?"

"I'm sorry." The priest quickly got ahold of himself. "Truly, it is *not* funny, but I couldn't help myself." He let out a long breath. "You see I was about to say that we did it for your protection."

Torin now understood Genero's jocular instinct, as he now shared it, but restrained himself, instead throwing the priest's earlier question right back at him: "What do we need to be protected from?"

"Chalmraik." Genero's face became grave. "You don't know what you're dealing with here, Lieutenants. We, at least, have faced Chalmraik before—we know what he's capable of."

"Everyone in Flingaria knows what Chalmraik is capable of," Danthres said. "That's not the point."

"It is very much the point! We could not get you involved!"

Danthres got up from the desk. "You arrogant piece of shit! We were involved the second Brightblade's body fell. You see, *this is what we do*. When there's a crime in Cliff's End, we are called upon to solve it. Anybody who interferes is obstructing us, and is liable for that." She walked over to the other side of the table, leaning over the priest, her left hand resting on the back of his creaky chair, her right on the table. From across the table, Torin could smell the not-quite-pleasant mix of tea and Jonas's wife's pastries on her breath, and he imagined that odd smell was even worse for the priest. In a quiet voice, she continued: "I'd be fully within my rights to throw you in the hole right now. And if you were *anyone* else, I would've done it an hour ago." She stood upright. "You're lucky, though. You're a guest of the Lord and Lady, the friend of two heroes, and a Temisan priest. If I even thought about it, I might as well pack my bags and leave the city-state all together. Between the local aristocrats and your religious superiors, I'd be up to my ass in trouble. And you know what?" She leaned back down again. "I'm *this close* to doing it anyhow, because you make me so sick. You're so self-righteous in your assuredness that you can do no wrong that you let three more people get killed and kept me from doing my job—you kept me from seeing that justice was served."

She walked away from the desk, turning her back on the priest.

Torin let the unpleasant silence hang in the air for

several seconds before saying, "You're free to go. If we have any other questions, we'll send someone for you."

Genero stood and looked at Danthres's back. "Lieutenant, you have to understand—"

"I don't have to understand a damn thing. Get out."

The priest took another long breath, then straightened his red robe and went toward the exit. Torin followed him. "I assume you will be remaining in the castle?"

Genero nodded. They came out into the squad room. "If I may ask, Lieutenant, what is your next step?"

"Some definitive proof that this really *is* Chalmraik would be a good start. Still, he seems to have covered his tracks quite well."

"Oh, for pity's sake," came a cantankerous voice from the far end of the squad room, "are you *still* on that imbecilic Chalmraik kick, ban Wyvald?"

Torin saw Boneen sitting at Dru and Hawk's desk. The three of them were going through a big pile of scrolls from the bootleg-spell bust. The guards of Dragon had caught their rapist-bootlegger running naked across the rooftops of Hranto's Way, and he was currently rotting in the hole. As far as Torin knew, no one had bothered to supply him with fresh clothes. Knowing how cold it got in the hole at night, this gave Torin happy thoughts.

Before Torin could reply to Boneen's question, Genero said, "There's nothing imbecilic about it, sir.

Chalmraik has obviously learned that we were pursuing him, and has taken steps to remove us from the playing field. He's not ready to make his move, so he needs to eliminate us before we can stop him from achieving full power."

"What utter nonsense." Boneen got up from Dru and Hawk's guest chair. "Even on the off chance that Chalmraik is alive, he can't possibly have committed these murders."

"Hey, we're workin' here," Dru said.

"Oh, give it a rest." Boneen waved his hand dismissively, not even looking at the lieutenant. "I told you before, there's no kind of magic that can cover up these murders so completely as these do."

Torin blinked. "Wait a moment, Boneen. Before, you said that no *practical* magic could do this." Even as he spoke, Danthres joined them from the interview room.

"Yes, I did say that."

Danthres looked at Torin and he saw the look on her face that indicated that she was following his train of thought. She asked, "What about impractical magic?"

Genero gave the lieutenants a quizzical look. "What?"

"It stands to reason," Torin said. "There are different types of—well, everything in the world, truly. So presumably there are types of magic other than that approved by the Brotherhood."

"A few." Boneen seemed to Torin to be reluctant

to admit this. "But only a total idiot would consider them."

"The world," Danthres said, "is well stocked with total idiots."

Boneen sighed. "I suppose, but—"

At the M.E.'s hesitation, Torin said bluntly, "Is there *any* kind of magic that can block a magical presence from a peel-back?"

Again, Boneen sighed. "Well, I suppose if you have someone stupid enough to indulge in chronotic magic . . ."

Frowning, Torin looked at his partner, who had as confused a look as Torin had ever seen on her face. That expression was shared by Dru, Hawk, and Genero, all of whom regarded the M.E. as if he had grown an extra limb.

Hawk finally said, "What in the name of all the oceans is cranking magic?"

"Chronotic magic," Boneen snapped. "I don't expect any of you to know about it—"

"Safe bet," Danthres muttered.

"—because not only is it restricted, it's insanely dangerous. Nobody's practiced it that we know of for about three hundred years, and that was an isolated case in which the wizard died a quick and painful death. The time before that was almost a thousand years ago, and almost wiped out all of Flingaria." Boneen grabbed the absent Iaian's chair from his desk and straddled it. "You're right, ban Wyvald, there are many types of magic, but most of them are difficult and dangerous. Chronotic magic is probably the worst of them. You see, it allows you to master the secrets of time."

"Speak Common, old man," Danthres snapped.

Genero said, "It means that the magic can be used to travel back and forth in time. You can go to the future or to the past."

"That's impossible," Dru said, scoffing.

"Oh, it *is* possible," Boneen said, "but extremely ill advised. You see—and I have to confess, I always found this ironic—the use of chronotic magic accelerates the aging process. Just as standard magic retards it—which is why I've been stuck on this miserable pile of mud for over two centuries—chronotic magic makes you age at a ridiculous rate. Anyone who used it would be dead of old age within a month. If the person who did this is using chronotic magic to mask his trail on four murders, then he may already be dead."

Torin stared at the M.E. incredulously. This changed *everything*.

Danthres snarled. "Why the *hell* didn't you mention this as a possibility sooner?"

"The same reason, Tresyllione, why I didn't mention an invisible tap-dancing goat as a possibility. In fact, given the choice between chronotic magic and the goat as likely options, I'd have gone with the goat."

Torin whirled on the priest. "Brother, a question: Was there anyone you encountered on your way here from Velessa, someone who might have carried a grudge against the seven of you?"

"Who'd be capable of this? Who'd be willing to indulge in so dangerous a form of magic to exact revenge? Not at all. We only came across some bandits, who were very surprised when they realized who, exactly, they were trying to rob," Genero added with a small smile, "and a couple of trolls, and that young mage."

Danthres blinked. "What mage?"

"A young man who was unregistered with the Brotherhood. I believe his name was Tesbi."

"Never heard of him," Boneen said.

"As I said, he was not registered."

"Which explains why I never heard of him," the M.E. said testily.

Torin yanked the conversation back on track. This was finally starting to come together. "Why did he attack you?"

"He wanted to steal Olthar's Healing Potion." Genero shook his head. "The boy was inept, and barely worth the effort for us to fight. Bogg wanted to kill him, but I stopped him."

"But he did cut his ear off," Danthres said quietly.

"Yes, the tip of it." Genero looked at Danthres. "He told you?"

"Can you describe the young man to Boneen here?" Torin asked.

Dru spoke up. "Hey, Torin, you mind? We got a case here."

"So do we," Danthres snapped.

"Yeah, well, this is gonna take forever to go through *with* Boneen. We gotta sort about three hundred spells before we give 'em to Ep to misfile, and I sure as shit don't want you takin' him off on yours to make ours take longer'n forever."

Danthres sounded wholly unsympathetic in her reply. "My heart bleeds."

Boneen turned to look at Dru. "I'm not a commodity to be traded. I'll get back to you two shortly, but if there's an unregistered mage wandering around, I need to know about it." The wizard stood up and walked over to the basin in the corner of the squad room, which Boneen sometimes used as a makeshift scrying pool. "Describe him."

For the next several minutes, Genero impressed Torin by providing a *very* detailed description of the young man, from the color of his eyes to the cleft in his chin to the shape of his nose. Within moments, Boneen had conjured an image based on that description.

The image was quite familiar to Torin. Or, at least, a version of it.

Genero nodded. "Yes, that's him. Well, except for the fact that the top of his left ear is now missing," he added with a smile.

"That is what I expected," Torin said. "Can you find this man?"

Emphatically, Boneen said, "I have every intention of doing so, ban Wyvald."

"Hey," Dru said, "what about us?"

"Your case'll keep." Boneen smiled insincerely. "The spells aren't going anywhere, after all. And if this young imbecile is unregistered, then I need to find him immediately."

"Not so young, I suspect," Torin muttered. "Find him quickly, Boneen."

Ten

I don't know this room.

Tesbi tried to focus his eyes, but they wouldn't cooperate. He knew he was in a strange place, and he even had some vague recollection of being brought here, but he couldn't figure out *why* he was here.

Or was it what he was doing here?

No, that doesn't make sense. Think.

He looked around the room. There wasn't much to see—just four walls, a door, and a lantern. He stared at the lantern for several seconds. His eyes watered for some reason. Eventually, he realized that it was because he was staring directly at the lantern's bright light, so he stared at something else instead.

The problem was, the room didn't really give him a lot to work with. Tesbi couldn't think of a room more boring than this.

Of course, he didn't remember most of the rooms he'd been in, so that didn't mean as much.

Something was carved in the table he sat at. They were lines of some sort. *I know what these are for.* He tried to focus on the lines. If he thought long and hard enough, he'd remember what the lines signified.

Writing? Is that what it's called?

The door opened, causing Tesbi to almost jump out of his chair. It hadn't occurred to him that the door might open.

Two people walked in. Tesbi was pretty sure he'd never seen them before. Or maybe they were the ones who brought him to this room. Then he realized that he couldn't recall what the two people who brought him to this room looked like. In fact, he wasn't entirely sure there were two of them—maybe there were three or only one. Or perhaps five.

No, not five. Definitely fewer than five.

One of the people had a beard so thick that Tesbi couldn't see his face. It reminded him of the old man—what was his name? *Why can't I remember his name?*

"What is this?" he asked the bearded man who looked like the old man, pointing at the lines.

"It's a table."

"I *know* it's a table." He frowned. The bearded man didn't just look like the old man, he looked like somebody else. "Do I know you?"

"Possibly. My name is Lieutenant ban Wyvald, this is my partner Lieutenant Tresyllione."

For the first time, Tesbi looked at the other person. "You're the ugliest woman I've ever seen."

"Thank you," the woman said. There was something weird about her tone of voice, but Tesbi couldn't figure out what it was.

He looked around. "I don't know this room."

"No reason why you should," said the bearded man. "You've never been here before. But you have spoken to me before, haven't you?"

"No."

"Really?"

"I don't think so." In fact, he had no idea. The image of the man's face came into his head, but not in this room. "It was in a bar. I think. You were surrounded by merchants. That was when I saw you. But it was a long time ago. I think."

"Do you remember what we talked about?"

"Couldn't have been anything important, or I'd remember it."

"Quite likely, yes. Your name is Tesbi, yes?"

"Is it?" He thought about it for a moment, and decided that it was. "Yeah, it is. How'd you know that? *I* wasn't even sure."

The bearded man, whose name Tesbi had already forgotten—*Binwivin? Something like that*—smiled. "We have our ways of learning information. Do you recall what we talked about?"

"We talked?"

"Yes, several times. Twice in the Dog and Duck, once at Jorbin's Way."

"Where's that?"

"Here in town."

"I've never been here before." Why was this man talking such utter nonsense? *And who is he, anyhow? I've never seen him before.*

"We were discussing murders—four of them in all."

Tesbi was suddenly frightened. "Someone's been killed?"

"Yes, four people—Gan Brightblade, Olthar loth-Sirhans, and two halflings named Mari and Nari."

Those names sounded familiar. "I've heard of them."

"They are heroes of Flingaria. You've probably heard bards sing about them."

"Don't like bards. They get everything wrong. You know what bards say? They say that magic is a wonderful thing. Well it isn't. Magic is rotten. Does things to you. Things they don't tell you about. And then they kick you out and won't let you do anything if you don't do it their way. Hate that." He blinked, and noticed that there were two people in the room. "Who're you?"

"Lieutenant ban Wyvald—this is my partner, Lieutenant Tresyllione."

"Do I know you from somewhere? I've seen you before." He looked up at the other one. "Not her—I'd remember a face as ugly as that."

The ugly woman started pacing behind the bearded man. Tesbi looked at the bearded man's beard. "You look like someone I know."

"We've spoken before—regarding several murders that have taken place."

Tesbi waved his hand. "No, no, no, not that—you look like the old man."

"What old man?"

"You wouldn't know him. For one thing, he's dead. Or, anyhow, he will be dead. When I kill him. But that hasn't happened yet. For all I know, he hasn't been born yet. I think. It's hard to keep it all straight." He looked down and noticed that there were strange lines on the table he was sitting at. "What're these?"

"Words," the bearded man said. "They're in Common."

"Right, right." He hadn't read Common in a long time. "I'm used to the sigils now. Been living with the sigils. And they're different, you know, from the regular magic. Any idiot can learn the regular magic. I'd been studying on my own, y'know. Had to, couldn't afford the damn fees the Brotherhood charges. Why do they do that?"

"Do what?" the bearded man asked after a moment.

"Take fees? I mean, if you know magic, and want to learn magic, shouldn't they just—just—just *teach* it? Why make you pay for it when you can't afford it? Especially if your mother's dying."

"Your mother's dying?"

"Was. Dead now. Dead for years. Well, actually, no, I guess not. Maybe dead a few months. Actually, she's probably not dead at all. But she will be soon. And if they'd just given me the Healing Potion . . ." Tesbi looked around. "I don't know this room."

"If who'd given you the Healing Potion?"

"What Healing Potion?"

"You said 'if they'd just given me the Healing Potion.' I'm wondering what Healing Potion you're speaking of."

For the first time, the ugly woman spoke. At least Tesbi thought it was the first time she said anything. "And who 'they' are."

Tesbi shook his head. "I'm so tired."

"I'm sure you are, Mr. Tesbi, but—"

"How'd you know my name?"

"You told it to me earlier."

"I did? I don't remember."

"But you do remember talking to me."

"I think so."

"Do you remember the people you tried to take the Healing Potion from?"

Tesbi shook his head. "I thought they were just seven folks. Traced the potion, figured I'd ambush 'em, take the potion. Didn't know."

"Didn't know what?" the bearded man asked after a moment when Tesbi stopped talking.

"You know what the worst thing was? They wouldn't let me do magic anymore. I tried to explain it to 'em, and then I tried to bargain with 'em, but it didn't work. You ever try bargainin' with a mage?"

The bearded man who looked like the old man smiled. "Not successfully."

"Hate wizards. I couldn't pay the fee, I couldn't save my mother, and then they just let her die and wouldn't let me do a thing about it. So I had to find someone to help me. He looked just like you."

"Who did?"

"The old man. He's dead now. Or he will be. And then I came back. Figured it was the least I could do for my mother." He looked around. "I don't know this room."

"So you found someone to teach you chronotic magic."

"What's that?"

The bearded man blinked. "The magic you learned."

"What I learned was time sorcery. That's what the old man called it, anyhow. I didn't know nothin' about it, but I wanted so much to learn magic, and those Brotherhood people wouldn't let me do anything else. Took me years to find someone who *would* teach me, but then he'd only teach me time sorcery."

"Why did you do it?"

Tesbi shrugged. "It's all I had."

"Didn't you know what would happen?"

"Yup. I'd go back in time and kill 'em all. I was

worried I'd have to find 'em all, but since I could go back in time, I could get 'em when they were all together after they met me. That'd show 'em. Show 'em that I wasn't just some idiot like that big guy said. That's why I killed him first, y'know. He said I was stupid. I ain't stupid. Just didn't have no money, so I couldn't learn right. No, I ain't stupid at all."

"Of course you're not."

Looking up, Tesbi was surprised to find that there were two people in the room with him, including the ugliest woman he'd ever seen and a familiar-looking man. "Who're you?"

"I'm Lieutenant ban Wyvald. This is my partner, Lieutenant Tresyllione."

"Didn't we speak at some bar?"

"Yes, we did. We were discussing the murders of Gan Brightblade and Olthar lothSirhans."

"They deserved to die. If they'd just given me the potion, my mother'd still be alive and none'a this would've happened."

"None of what would have happened, Mr. Tesbi?"

"How'd you know my name?"

"I know many things, Mr. Tesbi. I know that you attacked seven innocent people outside Cliff's End. I know that they would have killed you, but for the kindness of one of them—a Temisan priest. I know that another one of them cut off the top of your left ear. I know that you were turned over to the Brotherhood of Wizards, and you pled with them to let you study magic, or at the very least to heal your dying mother. They did neither, and prevented you from ever pursuing magic. After your mother died, you wandered Flingaria, trying to find someone who would teach you magic. But the Brotherhood's reach extends quite far, and you found every effort stymied. Until one day you found an old man with a thick beard who was willing to teach you forbidden magic—which would allow you to have your revenge on the seven people you believed responsible for ruining your life and keeping you from saving your mother. You went backward in time, using your new skills, and killed four of the seven people. And your use of that forbidden magic has aged you considerably and will kill you by week's end."

Tesbi frowned. "That's an interesting story."

"And a true one."

"It certainly sounds familiar. Reminds me of what happened to me once. My mother died, too, you know. Someone had a Healing Potion, but they wouldn't let me have it. I showed him, though—him and all his friends who thought I was an idiot."

The ugly woman spoke for the first time. Tesbi wondered why she hadn't said anything up until now. "Why didn't you go back further?"

He looked up at the woman, who was truly the ugliest creature he had ever laid eyes on—though he found he couldn't remember what anyone in the world other than the two people in front of him actually looked like. "Go back further than what?"

"Instead of going back in time to a point *after* Brightblade and the others stopped you, why didn't you go back to a time *before* then and prevent yourself from ever meeting them?"

Tesbi blinked once. Then he blinked again. Then he looked down at the writing on the table. Then he looked back up at the ugly woman. "That's an interesting idea. I hadn't thought of that. I'll have to do that." He looked back down at the writing. "That's Common, isn't it? I haven't read Common in so long. The sigils, you know, they've been everything." He looked around. "I don't know this room."

Danthres walked out of the interview room and proceeded to slam her fist into the wall.

"Feel better?" Torin asked as he followed her out.

"Not in the least, though it has succeeded admirably in making my hand hurt." She cradled her now-throbbing fist with her other hand.

Grinning, Torin said, "Well, that's something at least."

At the sound of footfalls, Danthres looked at the east-wing wall to see Osric walking out of his office, accompanied by Genero and Ubàrlig, who had remained in the squad room at the insistence of Sir Rommett. Danthres had decided that, of the many things she wished to do before she died, disemboweling the chamberlain had vaulted to near the top of the list.

"So it was him?" the captain asked.

Torin nodded. "Once I realized that my three witnesses who resembled each other were the same man aging at a great rate, it all fell together."

Osric fixed his one-eyed gaze on Jonas, who was shuffling parchments nearby. "Sergeant, get a guard up here to take this shitbrain to the hole. And have Boneen make sure the wards can work against his kind of magic."

"I don't think that will be an issue," Torin said.

"Why not?"

Danthres snorted. "Tesbi can't even remember his own name. That's probably why the killings stopped with the halflings—he's aged so much that his brain is addled."

Genero shook his head. "Such a waste."

"Waste, hell," Ubàrlig said. "We shoulda just killed 'im, like Bogg wanted. If we had, Gan and the others'd still be alive, and we'd be able to go and take Chalmraik down."

The priest rubbed his long chin-beard thoughtfully. "We cannot know that—and we cannot presume to know the course of the future."

"He does," Torin said. "Or did. I doubt you'll get anything coherent out of him now, but he lived the next few years as they were when Gan Brightblade and Olthar lothSirhans and Mari and Nari didn't die. If you fancy questioning him, you might find out how you would have fared. I'd be patient, though."

"Definitely," Danthres said. She had let Torin take the lead in the interview because she herself would have lost patience with his multiple digressions and constant repetitions. Danthres preferred the more conventionally stupid criminals they usually took on.

"No," Genero said. "Indulging in what-may-haves is not Temisa's way."

Ubàrlig barked a laugh. "I'd run outta patience two seconds in. Nah, we're better off not knowin'."

"You know what the absolute worst thing is?" Danthres asked suddenly.

Everyone turned to look at her at that.

She shook her head. "After all that, I almost feel sorry for the bastard. He just wanted to get his hands on a Healing Potion that he couldn't afford so he could save his mother's life. Oh, don't get me wrong," she added quickly at the incredulous looks that all save Torin gave her, "I think he should be thrown into the worst dungeon we have until the magistrate figures out the most painful way to have him executed. But it's not like he's the crazed killer or the megalomaniac we were all primed for. He's just some idiot who wanted to save his mother."

Ubàrlig walked to Danthres and looked up at her with steely eyes. "He's an idiot that killed four of my friends, including two of Flingaria's greatest heroes. That's all I care about."

With that, he left the squad room, presumably returning to his rooms in the north wing. Genero followed soon thereafter.

Danthres stared after them, shaking her head.

"Congratulations," Osric said after a moment. "You closed the case. And that means no more overtime. And I expect a good justification for the overtime you *did* claim."

"Oh come now, Captain, would we falsify an overtime request?"

Osric turned his back on Torin and Danthres as he headed back into his office. "You really don't want me to answer that question, ban Wyvald."

Chuckling, Torin turned to Danthres. "Drinks at the Chain tonight are on me."

Smiling, Danthres said, "That is the best offer I've gotten in weeks. Let's go."

Eleven

"You should've *seen* the look on his face when he found out about his brother," Iaian said after sipping some of his whiskey. "After he'd been going on for an hour about the 'house of ill repute,' when Amelie told him his brother still hadn't paid for the statuette he broke . . ." The old lieutenant trailed off, unable to contain his laughter.

Torin joined in the laughter, as did Dru and Hawk. Danthres, for her part, did manage a half-hearted smile.

They sat at their usual table in the back of the Old Ball and Chain, Iaian, Torin, and Hawk on the bench against the wall, Danthres and Dru in the two stools.

Danthres's lack of joviality concerned Torin. It had been a good day for all concerned. True, Dru and Hawk were still accounting for all the bootleg spells, but they had been able to stop at sundown, since the Lord and Lady weren't about to approve *more* overtime for the detectives, and Dru and Hawk weren't about to do extra mind-numbing work for free. But they had scored the biggest bootleg-spell bust in history, on top of nailing a serial rapist, and Iaian and Grovis had opened up yet another corruption case in Mermaid and stopped the bad glamours, and he and Danthres had closed the Brightblade murders. After all they'd been through, they had put down three major cases in the space of one day. Grovis, of course, had gone home—probably to express outrage to his brother over how his behavior was an affront to Ghandurha—but the others went straight to the Chain to celebrate.

But Danthres had not been celebratory, though she had joined in the toasts and been drinking along with the rest of them. Usually she was at her best when they put down a case.

"Honestly," Iaian said, "I think finding out his brother was a 'fornicator' hit him harder than Victro's kid did at the tavern."

Hawk laughed. "Please, man, *don't* be usin' that word."

"So Victro's kid's pickin' up where Dad left off?" Dru asked.

Iaian shook his head. "Nah, looks like the new sergeant is. He's just using Paol to get at Rai's old contacts. Same old shit in Mermaid. I hate it down there." He gulped down the rest of his whiskey. "I'm all for having the Brotherhood fireball the place and start over."

"Pretty good day, all 'round," Dru said. "We all put down our cases *and* Grovis looks like an even bigger idiot than usual."

Hawk grinned. "I think I was almost seein' a smile on the captain's face today."

"I know I saw one on mine." Dru looked at Danthres. "For one thing, he didn't have to fire you."

Danthres looked up from her ale. "And that makes you happy, does it?"

"Damn right. Long as you two're around, you'll get the pain-in-the-ass cases like Brightblade. You get fired, we'll get stuck with 'em."

Leaning back against the rear wall of the Chain, Iaian regarded Danthres. "You know, you don't *have* to go out of your way to piss people off. You could get a lot farther by just keeping your mouth shut and riding things out."

"What, like *you?*" Danthres spoke in a most contemptuous tone. "No, thanks."

"Danthres," Torin said in a cautionary voice. *Dammit, she should be happy—why is she picking a fight with Iaian, of all people?*

Luckily, Iaian wasn't taking the bait. "Hey, look, you don't want to take good advice, don't. But in two years, I get my twenty-five, and I'm outta here with a nice pile of coins in my money pouch. I'll be stunned if you make it to twenty the way you keep shitting in your soup."

"When you're already drinking shit soup, what difference does it make?" Danthres asked. She gulped down some more of her ale. "I suppose if you're only in it for the coin, that would be good advice."

Hawk looked at Danthres like she was insane. "What the hell other reason there be?"

Danthres gulped down more ale. Wiping the foam from her mouth, she looked around at the table. "Have any of you ever been to Treemark?"

Assorted negative answers went around the large table. Iaian muttered something about a cousin having visited there once.

Torin stared at his partner. "I've been there several times, as you well know. The surprise is that *you've* been there and haven't told me."

"There's a reason for that." Danthres did not actually look at Torin as she spoke to him, preferring to stare into her flagon of ale. "After I was forced to leave Sorlin, I went in search of my mother's family. There didn't seem to be much point in trying to find my father's relations, since they'd kill me the moment they looked at me, but I thought that perhaps my mother's people might take me in. When I was a girl, my mother told me that she had family in Treemark, so when I was—was forced to leave Sorlin as a teenager, that was where I went.

"I was surprised to find out that my mother's sister wasn't just a citizen of Treemark, she was an aristocrat. She lived in a huge mansion with dozens of servants. I was taken in immediately, with no question. My resemblance to my mother is fairly strong, so no one questioned that I was a member of the family. I was given my own room, my very own handservant—even some cousins who were about the same age as me.

"Not everyone was completely welcoming, of course, but my aunt Sarah gave me nothing but love, warmth, and affection—and, since she was Lady Cambri, her orders to treat me as one of the family were carried out to the letter."

"Cambri?" Dru leaned forward. "Hang on a sec, you mean you're related to the brick people?"

Sighing, Danthres said, "Yes, Dru, my mother's family are the brick people. May I finish my story now?"

Dru held up his hands in a defensive gesture. "Sorry. I just didn't think you were related to such heavy hitters."

"They're not heavy hitters, Dru, they're just people. And most of them didn't appreciate having me around. Still, they kept their tongues, because Aunt Sarah would be displeased if they didn't. And, as I learned *very* early on, no one short of King Marcus himself dared displease my aunt.

"Still, I found myself befriending the servants more than my assorted relations. They seemed more like real people to me, somehow—they had less of the artifice that is the hallmark of upper classes everywhere."

"That's the nice way of putting it," Iaian muttered from behind Torin. He looked up to see that Iaian had a fresh whiskey in his hand and was putting a flagon of ale in front of Danthres. Torin hadn't even noticed that his fellow detective had gotten up to go to the bar. "Figured you were gonna tell a long story, you'd need more lubrication."

Danthres looked up at the old lieutenant, and then down at his peace gesture, one that she should have offered him, not vice versa. Torin rarely saw his partner chagrined, but she looked that way now. "Thank you, Iaian. And I'm sorry, I—"

Iaian held up a hand as he sat back down. "Forget it. Just finish the story."

"Yeah," Dru said, "you got me hooked, too. Didn't know you had a deep dark past as an upper."

Snorting, Danthres said, "Hardly. Aunt Sarah *wanted* me to be part of the family, but it didn't take long for everyone to realize that I wasn't cut out for the aristocracy. I went through the motions, attended the dinner parties, met the important people, but mostly I stayed away from it all and talked with the servants. My own handservant was a kind young girl named Mista, and her sister Harra was the dining-room server."

"Wait a minute," Iaian said, putting his whiskey down after sipping it. "You were a teenager, you said?"

Danthres nodded.

"This wasn't when—?"

"Yes."

Torin frowned, then did the math in his head. "When they captured Bronnik."

Hawk squinted. "What, that serial-killer guy from twenty years back? Thought they be catchin' him in Iaron."

"No, it was in Treemark," Danthres said. "It was all anybody could talk about for weeks afterward. How depraved he was, just killing people without thought, and how awful it was, and how wonderful it was that he was finally captured. Which made what happened next so ironic."

In a gentle voice, Torin asked, "Which was?"

"One night, we were having a big dinner party for another one of my cousins, Sicund. He was returning from Iaron—he ran the family brickmaking concern up there. He had come home for a visit. We're having the party, and I'm bored out of my mind. I can't talk to the servants because that isn't done during dinner parties. So I'm studying the potted plants, trying to avoid eye contact with Sicund.

"So of course Aunt Sarah brought him over and introduced me to him. He was tall, skinny, supercilious, and walked with a cane for no good reason. He *did* have a limp, though how pronounced it was depended on the time of day and how much he'd had to drink. He claimed it was a war wound, but I don't believe he was ever in any kind of combat. I suspect he just used it to get sympathy from people and as a conversation starter. Probably helped him in his business."

Torin had a feeling he knew where this was going from the way she was telling the story. At once he both wondered and understood why she had never shared this tale with him before.

"Harra was supplying drinks. At one point she came in with fresh glasses for everyone. Sicund was declaiming about something—I wasn't really paying attention—and gesturing like mad, that damned cane of his flying all over the place. Harra had to duck to avoid being hit in the head, and she spilled her tray of drinks.

"Some of the drinks got on Sicund's clothes—and he was apparently wearing silk. He got furious and started beating on Harra with his cane for daring to get drinks on his outfit."

Dru blinked. "Holy shit."

"I tried to stop him, but he was insane with rage, and I was—a lot younger then. After he—after he hit her several times, he left the dinner party. I brought Harra up to her room and called for a healer, but there was nothing to be done. She died the next day."

"What happened to Sicund?" Torin asked, guessing the answer.

Danthres snarled. "Nothing. Oh, he left Treemark the next morning, but there was to be no punishment for him. If anyone asked, they were to say that Harra died in an accident and that Sicund was recalled to Iaron on business. Nobody seemed to care that Harra was dead. I went to Aunt Sarah and asked her why he was being allowed to get away with it.

"I swear, she looked at me blankly and said, 'Get away with what?' " Danthres looked around the table. "The idea that a servant's life was important didn't occur to her. She was only worried about the scandal. She used her wealth and her power to cover up the crime. After that, nobody ever even talked about Harra—not even her own sister." She gulped down the rest of the ale Iaian had brought her. "Harra deserved justice that day—she needed someone to speak for her, and no one did. Not even my aunt, whom I had mistakenly believed was different because she took me in." Danthres shook her head. "But she didn't take me in because she was a good person, she took me in because I was her sister's daughter, and I was therefore of her class and worthy of being included. Harra wasn't fortunate enough to have aristocrats for parents, so she did not get the same consideration. I swore I would never see that happen again, which is why I joined the Guard when I arrived in Cliff's End. *That's* why I don't give a shit about what people like Sir Rommett *or* the Lord and Lady think—because our job isn't to earn overtime and score points with the aristocracy or to mark time until retirement. We all do that, yes, but our *job* is to see that justice is done in an unjust world."

Torin gazed for many long seconds at his partner.

Then he raised his flagon and spoke in a quiet voice. "To justice."

Iaian raised his whiskey, and Hawk and Dru did the same with their flagons.

Danthres stared at Torin for a moment before raising her own flagon. "To justice."

After Torin gulped down his ale, Iaian said, "Oh, by the way, I didn't pay for that last flagon."

Blinking, Danthres said, "I beg your pardon?"

The old lieutenant pointed at another table. "He did. Said it was to congratulate you on a job well done."

Torin followed Iaian's gesture to see that he was pointing at Manfred, the talented young guard who had found her exotic the other night.

"Him again," Danthres said with disdain.

"I wouldn't blow him off," Iaian said. "He caught some kid in Unicorn who opened a portal in his parents' backyard. Brought a hobgoblin through."

Grinning, Torin said, "The best part is that the hobgoblin attacked the boy's mother—Elmira Fansarri."

Danthres made a face. "Isn't she the one that walks around with enough paint on her face to clog a drain?"

"That's the one." Torin chuckled. "Young Manfred stabbed the hobgoblin as it was trying to beat Madame Fansarri to death."

Iaian gestured expansively. "Hobgoblin blood *everywhere*. And those suckers bleed a nice slick green that takes forever to get out. Hell, only thing that really works is a Laundry Spell, and Fansarri's notorious for hating wizards, so she'll probably never get one."

Torin grinned. "Seems to me that someone who did that is worth at least thanking for the drink."

Danthres sighed. "You're determined to put me together with that idiot, aren't you?"

"I simply wish you to judge him fairly, and take note of his finer points. Besides, he's making such an effort." He leaned forward. "Would you rather I suggest you make up with Nulti?"

"I'm not even going to dignify that with a response." She turned and looked at Manfred. The youth raised his own wineglass in reply. In reply, she raised her own flagon, then looked back at Torin. "He's not *that* bad-looking."

Dru laughed. "See, *that's* the spirit. Y'only live once. 'Sides, us old married guys over here need you single types to live vicariously through."

"Yeah," Iaian added, "it's the only thing that gives our lives meaning."

"I was wondering that." Danthres actually smiled, which heartened Torin. Again she turned to look at Manfred. "Perhaps I will go over and give him my thanks."

Torin laughed. "Good. I think that is a fine way to end this day."

The next morning, Torin arrived at the squad room—a bit late, as usual—and noted that Danthres was still smiling. "Have a good night?" he asked.

Sergeant Jonas came out of his lair, shuffling his parchments, before Danthres could answer. "About time you arrived, ban Wyvald."

"Long morning," he said as he hung his cloak up next to Danthres's.

"Well, there aren't any pastries left. I told my wife to make fewer so you wouldn't get any if you came in late."

"Congratulations, Jonas," Danthres said, "you may have found an incentive for him to arrive on time."

The sergeant simply dipped his quill in an inkwell and looked at Dru and Hawk, their desk laden with scrolls. "You two are still on spell duty, yes?"

"Nice bit'a deducin' there, Sarge." Dru didn't even look up from the pile of scrolls on his desk.

"Yeah," Hawk said, "I figure we'll be through with these some time before Iaian retires. Maybe."

Dru snorted. "Nah, this is gonna take more'n two years."

"Fine," Jonas said, making a note on one of his parchments. "You two'll be okay with that. Iaian, Grovis, you'll have to talk to the magistrate today, obviously, then head down to Mermaid."

"Mermaid?" Iaian asked. "What for?"

"What do you think? You two were the ones who cracked the new corruption ring, so you two get to investigate it."

Iaian winced. "Oh, no."

"It will be our pleasure, Sergeant," Grovis said with an animated smile that made Torin wince. "Such malefactors amidst the Guard's own ranks cannot be tolerated. I can assure you that Lieutenant Iaian and I will spare no effort in weeding these bad apples from the mighty tree that is the Cliff's End Castle Guard."

Iaian glowered at his partner. "You don't weed apples." Then he looked at Jonas. "Why do *we* have to catch this one?"

"I told you, you two exposed it. It's procedure, you know that."

Sighing, Iaian said, "I just hate investigating other guards."

"Whyever for?" Grovis asked, sounding genuinely confused. "If they are abusing their authority—"

"Remember what I said yesterday about you not understanding, boy?"

"If you wish," Grovis said archly, "I shall take the lead in the investigation."

"In your dreams, boy." Iaian leaned back in his chair. "Mermaid. More damn fish."

"First, the magistrate," Jonas said. "And that leaves ban Wyvald and Tresyllione up next."

Danthres stood up. "What? Don't *we* have to talk to the magistrate, too?"

"What for?" Jonas seemed genuinely confused.

"Cast your mind back to yesterday," Torin said tightly. "You might recall that we incarcerated a murderer."

"Oh, that," Jonas said dismissively. "The Brotherhood's taking care of that."

"What?" Danthres and Torin said in unison.

"Yeah, some fellow from the Brotherhood came last night and took your man away." He ran through his parchments, and finally found one, which he put in front of Danthres. "They're taking care of it."

Reading the parchment aloud, Danthres said, "'The Brotherhood of Wizards claims jurisdiction over the murders of Gan Brightblade, Olthar loth-Sirhans, Mari, and Nari, as it involves the use of forbidden magicks. The Cliff's End Castle Guard is relieved of all responsibility.'"

"Hey, less paperwork," Iaian said.

"I'm sure," Grovis said, "that the Brotherhood will handle the case with all discretion."

"That's what I'm worried about," Danthres said.

"Everyone in the city-state's going to want to know when Gan Brightblade's murderer is going to be hanged," Torin said. "What're we supposed to tell them?"

From Osric's office came the captain's voice. "Whatever you want—except the truth, of course. Heaven forfend we tell anyone someone's using crappy magic, or whatever it's called."

Torin turned to see that Genero and Ubàrlig were standing behind Osric. "It is outrageous," the priest said. "Our friends killed, and *this* is the justice we receive?"

"Well, Brother," Danthres said, "if you had been

a bit more forthcoming with us in the first place—"

"It wouldn't have made a difference," Torin said with a sigh. "It just would have meant the Brotherhood would've stuck their beards into it sooner."

"By the way, that isn't all this little directive says." Danthres read on. "'Any concerns about Chalmraik the Foul should be disregarded. Chalmraik is even less of a concern than ever he was, and any pursuit of this deceased wizard will be viewed as a hostile act by the Brotherhood.'" She looked up at Genero. "I think that last was directed at you two."

"This is outrageous," Genero repeated. "We should—"

The dwarf put a hand on the priest's arm. "Not do a damn thing. What're you, stupid? The Brotherhood's threatened us; Gan, Mari, Nari, and the stupid Ear are all dead. What're we supposed to do—find Chalmraik and hope Bogg drowns him in drool? That's about our best bet now, Genero."

Torin smiled grimly. "You should listen to the general, good Brother Genero. He is wiser than he looks."

"Well, that wouldn't take much," Danthres muttered.

"Perhaps you are right," Genero said.

Osric stared at the priest with his one good eye. "He's very right. There's been enough foolishness in my city these last few days, I'm not about to let you add to it, even if you are the Lord and Lady's guests. Do I make myself clear?"

"Yes, you do, Captain," Ubàrlig said quickly before Genero could say anything. "Let's go, old friend."

Torin watched them depart the squad room. "Those two are going to have a lot to work out, I think."

Danthres snorted. "It's what they get for trying to take the law into their own hands."

"How profound," Torin said dryly.

"It's true! If they just trusted people to do their jobs instead of deciding they needed to determine the fate of Flingaria themselves, this would never have happened."

"Yes, but—"

"All right, that's enough." Osric interrupted what Torin thought was going to be a very good point. "Back to work. Jonas?"

Jonas shuffled more parchments, even as Osric went back into his lair.

Torin looked expectantly at Jonas. "So what do we have?"

"Well, Mermaid's reporting a rash of robberies of some merchants down by the docks. You two'll have to check that out. Oh, and a theatre company's coming into town tonight."

Torin winced. "Oh, no."

"That's right," Jonas said with a nod, "that means increased crowding, more bar brawls, more traffic on Sandy Brook, and possible riots if the performances are lousy enough."

"It's not the same people who did *The Ballad of King Ytrehod,* is it?" Torin asked.

Jonas shuffled his parchments. "No, I don't think so."

"Then there's a chance it'll be tolerable."

"Oh, and the Temisan church is glowing."

Danthres chuckled. "Brother Genero's outrage, no doubt."

"Maybe, but you never know with gods. Dragon's put some extra patrols around there, just in case."

Rising from his chair, Torin immediately retrieved his cloak, wondering why he'd bothered to take it off in the first place. He also grabbed Danthres's. "Come on," he said, "let's head down to the Docklands, see what we can find out about these robberies."

Also getting up, Danthres said, "Might as well, yes, since our quadruple murder has been yanked out from under us."

"Speaking of which," Torin said, "you still owe me three coppers."

"What?" Danthres asked, sounding confused.

"Brightblade's murder. You bet me three coppers it was a bar brawl."

"Are you still harping on that?"

" 'Harping'? Might I remind you that *you're* the one who made the wager in the first place?" Torin shook his head as they moved toward the castle's exit. “Tell you what, I’ll forgive the debt if you tell me what, precisely, happened last night.”

Danthres smiled again. It looked good on her. “I’ll think about it.”

And with that, they proceeded into the city-state of Cliff’s End to do their jobs.

About the Author

Keith R.A. DeCandido is a white male in his mid-thirties, approximately 185 pounds. He was last seen in the wilds of the Bronx, New York, though he is often sighted in other locales. Usually he is armed with a laptop computer, which some have classified as a deadly weapon. Through use of this laptop, he has inflicted dozens of novels, short stories, comic books, nonfiction books, eBooks, and anthologies on an unsuspecting reading public. Most of these are set in the milieus of television shows, movies, and comic books, among them *Star Trek* (in all its incarnations), *Buffy the Vampire Slayer*, *Farscape*, *Gene Roddenberry's Andromeda,* Marvel Comics, *Xena, Doctor Who,* and many more. He has also perpetrated the acclaimed original science fiction anthology *Imaginings*. *Dragon Precinct* is his first original novel, though we have received information confirming that another short story involving Torin,

Danthres, and the city-state of Cliff's End will be appearing in the 2004 anthology *Murder by Magic*, edited by Rosemary Edghill. If you see DeCandido, do not approach him, but call for backup immediately. He is often seen in the company of Terri Osborne and two cats who go under the street names of "Mittens" and "Marcus." A full dossier can be found at DeCandido.net, with further information at KRADfanclub.com.